RIDE BACK TO REDEMPTION

After a bank raid robbed him of his wife and unborn child, Jeff Warrinder, sheriff of Redemption, ended up a drunken no-hoper. Working off a debt to Cassie Hanson, he gets tangled up in her feud with Bull Krantz. Meanwhile, the new sheriff is in deep trouble, whilst Krantz's gang of outlaws is after Jeff's blood. If he's ever to make the ride back to Redemption, Jeff must overcome his own demon: the one that comes in a whisky bottle.

Books by Eugene Clifton
in the Linford Western Library:

HANG THE SHERIFF HIGH

EUGENE CLIFTON

◆

RIDE BACK TO REDEMPTION

Complete and Unabridged

LINFORD
Leicester

First published in Great Britain in 2006 by
Robert Hale Limited
London

First Linford Edition
published 2007
by arrangement with
Robert Hale Limited
London

British Library CIP Data

Clifton, Eugene
 Ride back to Redemption.—Large print ed.—
 Linford western library
 1. Western stories
 2. Large type books
 I. Title
 823.9'2 [F]

 ISBN 978–1–84617–660–9

Published by
F. A. Thorpe (Publishing)
Anstey, Leicestershire

Set by Words & Graphics Ltd.
Anstey, Leicestershire
Printed and bound in Great Britain by
T. J. International Ltd., Padstow, Cornwall

This book is printed on acid-free paper

1

Ignoring her husband's proffered hand, Sarah stepped up to the buckboard's bench seat. 'I wish you'd stop your nonsense, Jeff. Doctor Michaels says I'm fine, and the way this baby's kicking there's nothing wrong with him either. I could walk to the store, it's only a step.'

'Man's got a right to look after his wife,' Jeff Warrinder replied, climbing up beside her and unhitching the reins from the brake. 'Still not sure this town's a fit place for a lady to go out alone.'

'Nonsense.' Her dimples showed. 'You've got it hand-tamed.'

'Maybe. Anyway, it's kinda warm to be walking up that hill.'

Sarah sighed. 'Wearing that badge makes you a sight too fond of having your own way. Bossing folks gets to be a habit.' The smile on her face belied the sting of her words.

Jeff glanced around; it was real quiet down here at the junction of Ford Street and Main. As the bay mare pulled the buckboard into motion he leant across and gave his pretty wife a kiss, lingering over it until she pushed him away with a laugh, her cheeks flushed. 'And that's no way for the sheriff to behave right out in the open where everyone can see.'

The crack of a shot broke the afternoon silence. Jeff frowned, staring up towards the centre of town. Redemption was built on a sloping bluff, narrowing towards the top at the northern end where the oldest buildings, including the Redemption hotel, the store, the bank and the sheriff's office, were located. 'Maybe I'd best turn around and take you back home.'

'It'll just be one of Bull Krantz's boys whooping things up,' Sarah said mildly. 'Don't fuss.'

'I guess.' Jeff clicked his tongue to the

chunky bay mare between the shafts, urging her to get a move on up the hill. Only two roads led in and out of Redemption. The high cliffs of the bluff made it impossible to approach the town from the north or the east. To the west it was flanked by the river. Down beyond the cabin where the Warrinders lived, Ford Street led to the only safe crossing in ten miles, while a wider track snaked away south towards Burville, the county seat.

'Water's high,' Jeff commented, half turning to look back at the river then giving his full attention to the horse as the road grew steeper and it leant to its work. 'You figure — '

The crack of another shot from somewhere ahead cut his words off short. 'I'd best put you down,' Jeff said. 'That's trouble.'

'No, stop fussing. I'm fine. Life's been a little quiet lately.' Her cheek dimpled again. 'I wouldn't object to watching you tear a strip off some of the Double Bar K boys.'

He hesitated. 'I may have quieted this town down some, but I'm not so sure about you.' Two more blasts exploded into the warm afternoon air. Jeff slapped the reins down on the bay's back. 'Hold on then, Sarah.'

The buckboard swayed and bounced as the horse powered its way up the slope. There was a flurry of movement ahead. More shots rang out. A mule tied up outside the store squealed suddenly and fell, legs kicking. By the hotel something lay crumpled on the steps, while on the left-hand side of the road a tangle of horses wheeled outside the bank.

As the buckboard drew closer, two riders pulled clear of the confusion, angling their mounts round to face them down the hill. A rangy brown horse with an empty saddle wheeled to follow, leaping clear over a body that lay sprawled in the street. A red stain was spreading into the dirt. The fallen rider's hat rolled away to reveal that he had a blue bandanna tied over the lower part of his face.

A man stood by a loaded wagon outside the grain store, his back to the advancing buckboard, all his attention fixed on the two riders as they galloped flat out towards him. After a second's hesitation he reached for something alongside his load. He straightened with a shotgun in his hands and took two steps out in to the road.

'That's Steve Hanson,' Sarah said.

'Dammit!' Jeff reached one hand to the floor, feeling for his rifle, pulling it clear and laying it across his knees. He lashed the bay horse with the reins. 'Crazy young fool!'

The tragedy unfolded, slow and inevitable as the passage of time. People peered from windows and shop doorways; these moments would be engraved forever on Redemption's memory. The riders were spurring their horses hard, but one of them held a rifle steady in his grasp as he leant into the motion.

They didn't hear the shot over the

rumbling protests of the buckboard and the drumming of hoofs, but Steve Hanson reeled and fell, and he didn't move again. The outlaw hadn't slowed, nor had he lowered his gun, seeking now for another target, seeing the man in the buckboard coming straight at him, maybe even spotting the badge on his chest.

Sheriff Jeff Warrinder hauled on the reins so hard the bay sat back on its haunches; if the hill hadn't been so steep the buckboard might have run on and over its heels. The two riders were almost upon them, but Jeff had spoiled the gunman's aim.

He pushed Sarah roughly down in front of the buckboard's seat. The rifle slid from his lap and she grabbed and held it; he needed both hands for the reins. Jeff's back felt horribly broad as he kept the animal turning, the wagon's wheels spinning and sliding in the dust, shaving so close to the sidewalk that a few splinters flew off the steps outside the haberdasher's shop.

In a breathless moment that seemed to last forever the two men had passed them and were galloping down the hill. People were emerging from the store and the hotel, some of them running for their horses; it wouldn't take the townsmen long to mount up and give chase. If the bank robbers headed for the ford with the river running so fast they'd be caught before they reached midstream. Most likely they knew that, and they'd go south.

'I'll be needing that rifle,' he said, glancing at his wife as he lashed at the bay again. 'You all right?'

She returned his look with a nod, a light in her blue eyes that owed nothing to fear. The man who shot Steve Hanson was twisting in the saddle. A bullet shrieked past Jeff's ear. He ducked involuntarily and bit back a curse.

There was a bend ahead where the road forked. To the right the trail went past the house they'd left just a few minutes ago, then down to the ford, while to the left it snaked between the telegraph office and the cattleman's association on its way out of town. The riders leant into the bend and headed for open country.

Jeff hauled left-handed and the bay's head came round reluctantly; the road to the right led back to its stall, away from this sudden madness. Slipping the reins over his shoulder and around his left arm to free his hands, Jeff reached for the rifle. He snapped off a couple of shots, and thought he saw blood spray from one of the horses.

It was all too much for the bay. It flung up its head and tried to turn for home, nearly dragging Jeff off the seat. He dropped the rifle and grappled with the reins but the buckboard was slewing wildly to the left.

There was a drop at the side of the road; it had been levelled to raise it above the last fall of the slope from the bluff down to the plain.

For a split second it looked as if they'd make it. The horse's hoofs stayed on the hard-baked dirt. But the buckboard was still skidding sideways, the left wheels trying to run on thin air. With a tearing crash the little wagon turned over, the horse snorting in terror as it was taken along for the ride. A splintered shaft plunged into its belly like a spear as it landed beneath the ruin and the beast screamed.

His hands clutching frantically for his wife, Jeff was flung clear, to roll a couple of times in the dust. He came half to his feet before he'd stopped tumbling and scrambled back to where Sarah lay. She was staring up at the sky, a look of surprise in her forget-me-not blue eyes. Jeff laid a hand gently against her cheek. The pretty head lolled, too quick, too easy. Even as she met her husband's look life fled from her gaze. Her neck was broken.

Numbly he reached out to close the dead eyes. He wanted to throw back his head and howl like an animal. Hoof-beats sounded on the road behind him. He looked round. It was his deputy,

Nate Grundy, his big black coming to a sliding halt. Sheriff Warrinder stared at the young man in blank anger then leapt to his feet.

'Get off that horse.'

Grundy hesitated, glancing to the south where the two riders were spurring into open country, then looking down at Sarah Warrinder's body. 'There's folk on the way. We'll see to it, Jeff; they won't get away.'

Sheriff Warrinder was at his side, one hand already on the rein. 'I gave you an order, Deputy. The horse!'

Grundy was barely out of the saddle before the sheriff was on the horse's back, his right hand dragging Grundy's Winchester repeater from its holster. As his heels drummed at his mount's sides Jeff Warrinder heard a solitary shot ring out behind him. Nate had put the bay out of its misery. He felt a momentary pang of jealousy; nobody would do the same for him. Then self-pity was forgotten. There was a job to be done.

The sheriff drove the horse to a wild

gallop, flattening himself on its neck, gaining inch by inch on the two riders as they fled from his fury. His whole existence narrowed down to this one moment, this one purpose. The Winchester felt heavy in his hand. He almost let it go; he didn't need a weapon, his wrath alone would suffice to see that justice was done.

A mile sped by beneath the flying hoofs, then another. The gap was closing, one horse flagging. Jeff Warrinder noted the crazy motion of the horse's black tail as it stumbled wearily; there was a wide splash of blood darkening its quarters. The animal was almost ready to drop.

The fugitive turned in the saddle to look back, his mouth opening in astonishment as he saw how close his pursuer had come; panic clear in his eyes when he realized the sheriff couldn't be outrun. Warrinder gained another couple of yards as the man drew his six-gun, but he made no attempt to lift Nate's Winchester, letting it hang lax in his grasp.

Shots spattered past him. Warrinder doubted he'd have felt a thing if one of them had found its mark; he was beyond feeling. Raking the horse's sides he felt the big black respond. His quarry was only five yards away. Then four. A last shot whined by and the six-gun was empty. With a howl of fear and rage the rider dropped the useless weapon back into his holster and bent low to urge the wounded horse to one last effort.

Sheriff Warrinder rode up alongside. He wanted to beat this man to a pulp, but some scrap of common sense remained; there was still the second rider, the one who'd gunned down Steve Hanson. Riding a fine-boned chestnut he was holding his lead. With something like reluctance Warrinder lifted the rifle to his shoulder.

Finding himself staring down the gun's muzzle the big man heaved on the reins at the exact instant when the bullet spat from the rifled barrel. The shot took him in the side and he tipped and fell.

When the sheriff looked back a moment later the horse was standing with its head down, blowing hard, while the man lay on the ground, not moving. The drum of many hoofs signalled that Grundy had gathered up more men for the pursuit. Satisfied, Warrinder turned his attention to the man on the chestnut, still in front of him and turning in the saddle, trying to sight down the long barrel of his rifle.

The first bullet threw up a spurt of dust under the black's hoofs. The second sang past Jeff's ear. He dropped the Winchester. For an insane moment he thought he could hear Sarah's voice, that half-amused, half-irritated tone she used when she was scolding him.

'Are you *trying* to get yourself killed, Jeff Warrinder?'

She'd got it right. He was. But not yet.

The chestnut slowed. A man couldn't shoot accurately and kick on his horse at the same time. From some inner reserve the big black Warrinder rode found an ounce more effort, flattening a little more, stretching its neck and galloping as if the hounds of Hell were on its heels.

The rifle barked just one more time. Warrinder felt a draught of wind stroke across the top of his head. He didn't spare it a thought. The two horses were almost neck and neck. The click as the rifle's hammer came down on an empty chamber sounded clear above the drum of hoofs. Yelling a curse at fate, the man flung the gun at the sheriff's head. It missed by a foot and cartwheeled away from them.

The blood was singing in Warrinder's ears. Death was so close he could smell it. Reaching out a hand he grasped his quarry by the wrist. He pulled with all his considerable strength. Both men and horses fell, a spectacular jumble of tumbling bodies and flailing legs. For the second time that day Warrinder was somersaulting, trying to hold on to something, reluctant to let go . . . He heard the crack as the bones in the man's arm splintered, bringing a yelp of pain. Still he held on.

Hot dust swept into Warrinder's face, choking him, blinding him. He rolled to his knees and breathed deep of the dirty air then opened his eyes, ignoring the grit searing his eyeballs. A drift of oversized snowflakes scattered down around him. The money the men had stolen from the bank was billowing from a torn saddle-bag as the chestnut scrambled to its feet and limped away.

Warrinder's prey lay half beneath him, pain-dimmed eyes staring up in terror, his uninjured hand groping for the pearl-handled six-gun at his side. With slow deliberation Warrinder reached over and drew the pistol before the man could reach it.

The world turned dark. To the end of his life Jeff Warrinder would swear he couldn't recall what happened in those few minutes out on the Burville road. It was a lie; he would never forget a single second. One blow with the six-gun's butt broke the bank robber's hand. After that Warrinder threw the weapon aside. There was an intense satisfaction in pounding his fists into unresisting flesh and bone, mashing the man's face until it was a featureless mask. At the end he lifted the mutilated head and smashed it down on to the ground, over and over until it split open like an overripe fruit.

No sound reached him. He didn't hear the injured man's screams as they faded into silence, nor the rattle of his last breath. Nor did he see the townsmen as they came to surround him. He was still pounding at the dead body when Nate Grundy grabbed hold of his arm. Screaming defiance he turned to tackle this new enemy. Jim Ormond, Redemption's blacksmith, came to Nate's aid. Between them the two men pinioned their sheriff's arms and dragged him away.

Jeff Warrinder sagged, spattered with blood, his knuckles skinned raw. When they let him go he dropped to his knees and buried his head in his hands.

2

'Dirty double-crosser!' The words slurred from the mouth of the man clutching at the hitching rail. He'd lost his hat, and his long hair hung lank over his eyes to tangle with his shaggy beard. His clothes were filthy enough to shame a cowboy coming back from a three-month cattle drive. Despite the support he swayed precariously as he made a clumsy lunge forward. 'Godamm thief!'

Sheriff Nate Grundy stepped back, easily dodging the haymaker aimed at his chin, leaving his attacker to collapse heavily to the ground, half on and half off the sidewalk.

'Take it easy,' the young sheriff said resignedly. 'Did you have to pick a fight with Rupe Krantz? His pa's likely to press charges this time, and I'm running out of excuses. Why can't you get drunk quiet-like?'

There was no response but a fuddled growl. Grundy sighed, leaning down to pull the drunk to his feet. 'I'll quit wasting my breath; you're way too full of Pusey's firewater to hear a word. Let's get you inside. Try not to puke in the office this time, Jeff. Abe's getting tired of cleaning up after you.'

He manhandled his burden up the steps and through the office door.

'Abe? Get out here.'

Deputy Abe Bozeman appeared at the door that led to the cells. The old man glanced at the drunkard and frowned. 'Not again. We ain't got no room.'

'What? I've only been gone an hour,' Grundy said. 'Where d'you find some-body to lock up that quick?'

'Didn't find nobody. Bull Krantz came with some of his boys just after you left. They found 'emselves a rustler.'

'And they brought him in?' Grundy eased Jeff Warrinder to the floor, where he was instantly and comprehensively sick. 'Oh, Jeez!'

It was a few minutes before Nate Grundy got back to the subject of the occupied cell, by which time Warrinder was curled up under the solid oak desk that had once been his own, his eyes closed and his shaggy head resting on a bruised fist.

'Don't tell me old man Krantz is getting soft in his old age?' Nate glanced at the figure lying at his feet. 'Even Jeff could never keep Bull from taking the law into his own hands. If the Krantzes found 'emselves a rustler I'm surprised they didn't string him up.'

'Guess they would've,' Bozeman replied. 'Only it ain't a he: it's Cassie Hanson.'

The sheriff looked at his deputy in disbelief. 'Are you telling me you've got a woman locked up back there?'

'Didn't have no choice.' Old Abe Bozeman refused to meet his boss's eyes. 'Bull swore he'd caught her red-handed with a dozen head of his prime steers. Had three of his hands along to back him up. Says if we don't keep that gal off'n his land he'll let 'em string her to the nearest tree, fee-male or no.'

'One hour,' Nate said. 'I was only away for one hour! We can't put a woman in jail alongside a man like Ross Cord.'

'I wouldn't do that,' Abe said hurriedly. 'No siree. I minded what you told me. Didn't go near Cord when his dinner was sent over from the hotel, I pushed his food tray in with my foot an' all, never opened the door. Mrs Hanson's in the other cell, an' I rigged up a blanket to keep things kinda decent for her.'

'But . . . ' Grundy ran out of words. He pushed through the door to the cells behind his office. Through the right-hand grille facing him he could see Cord, lying stretched out on the bunk, his head propped against the wall and his eyes fixed unblinkingly on the sheriff as he approached. To the left, with a blanket tied from the bars at the narrow window across to the door,

Cassie Hanson stood with her arm through the grille, caught in the act of inserting a hairpin into the lock.

'And about time!' She pulled her hand back through the bars and replaced the hairpin in the untidy knot of hair on the nape of her neck. Cassie Hanson was a head and a half shorter than the sheriff. He recalled the way she'd looked a year ago, a pretty girl driving into town alongside her new husband to fetch their supplies, or dressed in her Sunday best for church.

Right now she barely looked like a woman, her curves hidden in a man's ragged mackinaw that was held tight around her waist with a piece of twine. Reaching out to the bunk behind her she picked up a battered old felt hat and jammed it on her head. 'You'd better let me out of here right now, Nate Grundy.'

'Bull Krantz says you rustled some of his beef.'

'Rustled!' She grabbed the bars and shook them angrily. 'How else am I supposed to survive when he helps himself to all my young stock? I must have lost more than half this year's breeding to him.'

'No law to stop him putting his brand on a few clearskins, not if they're on open range.'

'I don't deny we were late with the branding at the Lazy Zee, but by the time I started there must've been a hundred head of mine on the wrong side of the river. Anyone but Bull Krantz would have driven them back, but he just put his mark on my young stock alongside his own. Maybe he had his hands fetching them in the first place; I wouldn't put it past the mean old buzzard.'

'Nothing I can do about that unless you've got some proof, Mrs Hanson. This feud won't do anybody no good. In a day or two I'll go talk to Krantz. Meantime I'll let you go if you promise to stay away from his cattle.'

The young woman glowered at him. 'I will not. When Steve was alive Bull wasn't a bad neighbour. He was high-handed, with worse manners than a mule, but we got along well enough. Now he's trying to drive me out of business. Folks around here pay you to keep the law, Mr Grundy, and it's not right letting Bull Krantz treat me that way. If you haven't got the guts to tackle the man just let me go and talk to him. I'll make him see reason.'

'I can't do that, Mrs Hanson. If it's true you drove some of Bull's steers off his range that's a hanging offence. We'll get it smoothed over somehow, but right now you'd best stay right where you are.' As she opened her mouth to protest he turned on his heels and returned to the office. He was back in less than a minute, dragging the senseless form of a man by the shoulders.

'Step back, ma'am. Abe, get the door open. I'm sorry to do this to a lady, but there's no place else I can put him. Jeff's gonna be keeping you company tonight.' He laid the unconscious man on the floor at the back of the cell. 'Abe'll put a chair right out here to keep an eye on the both of you, all decent and proper, though I'd say the roof blowing off is more likely than Warrinder waking up before midday.'

Cassie Hanson bit her lip but said nothing. The sheriff backed out of the cell and waited till his deputy had locked the door. Then he went into the office, coming out with the visitor's chair. 'You heard me, Abe. You set yourself down.'

The old man shrugged, casting an uneasy glance at Ross Cord. The robber returned the look, a slight grin on his pale lips. 'Sure ain't fair,' the outlaw drawled. 'Can't see the little lady from here.'

'Shut your mouth, Cord,' Nate Grundy said curtly, 'or I'll shut it for you. Those marshals from Burville better get a move on and fetch you out of here soon; don't reckon I'll ever be rid of the stench.'

⋆   ⋆   ⋆

It was late, several hours past midnight. Cassie Hanson lay on the bunk staring at the dark sky through the tiny window. Across the cell a soft rhythmic snore issued from where the drunken Jeff Warrinder lay. Twice she'd got up to poke him in the back, bringing the noise to a halt for a while, but now the sound was eclipsed by the rasping vibrations of old Abe's throat as he dozed, and she'd given up hope of sleeping. In the next cell she could hear Ross Cord pacing the distance from the door to the window and back again, soft-footed as a cat.

From the front office came the creak of wood then suddenly a sharper noise, impossible to pin down. Abe Bozeman snorted and shifted in his chair, but no more sounds disturbed the night. He settled again. His snores almost covered the slight chink of the chimney being lifted off a lamp, and the scrape of a light being struck.

Some instinct made Cassie tuck her head down and feign sleep, leaving a space so she could see out from under the blanket. The door from the sheriff's office opened and light spilled into the cells. Ross Cord stopped pacing, his footfalls halting abruptly, the bars giving out a faint musical ring as he clutched at them. 'About time,' he hissed. 'Get rid of him.'

A shape moved across in front of the cells. There was a strange rasping sound, then the most terrible noise Cassie had ever heard. Abe Bozeman gave a choking moan, his breath bubbling in his throat. There was a crash as he and the chair fell together. Cord swore. 'Watch the noise. Finish it!'

'No need. He's done for.'

Cassie bit hard at her lip to keep herself from crying out. The old man lay only feet away from her on the stone floor, blood pumping from the gaping red slash across his neck. She shut her eyes, but she couldn't keep out the sounds of the old deputy's dying. With a jangle of keys and a moment later a rush of footsteps, Ross Cord was freed.

'Let's get out of here.' It was the voice of the man who'd spoken before, the man who had just killed Abe Bozeman.

'Wait. Gimme those keys. And hand me the light.' Cord said.

Cassie screwed her eyes shut, willing the other man to refuse and hurry him away.

'Why?'

'Just curious.' The door of her cell was unlocked and the blanket was ripped off her. She opened her eyes and stared up into the square-jawed stubbly face she'd glimpsed briefly when Abe had brought her in. Ross Cord smiled down at her, showing a gap in his brown-stained teeth.

'Can see why they wasn't gettin' too excited, but I reckon you'd clean up fair enough.' He reached for her hand and pulled her to her feet. Cassie glared up at him, keeping her gaze resolutely away from the figure lying in the passageway.

'You crazy?' It was a tall, thin man

who spoke, standing up against the bars, his face hidden under a grubby bandanna. This was the killer, the man with the knife. In the light of the single lamp she could just see the shape of another man in the door of the office beyond.

'We'll be hidin' out for a month at least. When they see what you done to the old man the posse won't give up easy. Gets kinda lonely in them hills.' Cord made to drag her out of the cell but Cassie forestalled him, tugging her hand from his and moving fast to lead the way.

'The noise you're all making we'll be lucky to get clear of the town before the sheriff comes after us,' she said.

Cord chuckled softly. 'Am I gettin' this right? You wanna come?'

'Didn't you hear what the sheriff said? Nobody crosses Bull Krantz; he's the biggest rancher in these parts. If I'd been a man they'd have put a rope round my neck already. Since I'm a woman they'll give me a trial and make it legal, but I'll still end up dead.'

'Who's that?' The tall man had noticed the man on the floor of her cell. 'Sleeps sound, don't he?'

'Man by the name of Warrinder,' Cord said.

The man shook his head, pulling the bandanna down from his mouth. 'That don't make sense. Warrinder was the sheriff here. The lousy bastard killed my brother Job. Shot him, after him and the Hausel boys hit the bank. I heard it took Job a week to die.' He went into the cell and grabbed the unconscious man by the shoulders, shaking him roughly.

'That's no sheriff.' The man who'd stayed by the office door spoke for the first time. 'Looks more like a mountain man.'

'One way to be sure,' Cord said. 'The deputy did a lot of braggin'. He was tellin' me about a sheriff here before the one they got now, figure the name could have been Warrinder. He said the man killed Billy Silver back in Laredo.

Took a slug in the left shoulder doin' it. Wound like that leaves a scar. Take a look, Brodie.'

The thin man bent to rip the filthy shirt.

'It's him right enough,' Brodie said, a humourless grin lifting the corners of his mouth. 'Job would just love to see this, reckon I get to set things square tonight.'

'Thought you were in a hurry to leave,' Cord said.

'Not just yet. Me an' Warrinder's got some unfinished business.'

3

Brodie held his captive one handed and struck him hard across the face. Jeff Warrinder grunted as his head snapped round with the force of the blow but he didn't wake.

'Dammit!' The outlaw dropped him and aimed a couple of vicious kicks at his ribs. When the unconscious man still showed no sign of life, Brodie drew his knife, already stained with Abe Bozeman's blood.

Cassie Hanson gave a shrill laugh. Brodie turned and glared at her. 'You findin' this funny?'

'Sure.' She struggled to keep her voice steady. With one man lying dead at her feet it somehow seemed desperately important to save Jeff Warrinder's life. 'He's been trying to drink himself to death ever since he got his wife killed. Reckon he'll be real grateful to you for making things so easy for him.'

'He killed his wife?' Cord was curious. 'How come?'

'She fell out of his wagon and broke her neck when he chased after the men in that bank raid. The one where his brother got shot,' Cassie replied, nodding at Brodie. 'The sheriff blamed himself.'

'That's some kind of justice.' The man in the doorway shifted restlessly. 'Time we got out of here, Brodie. Do it an' let's go.'

'No.' Brodie scowled and dragged the still-unconscious Warrinder out of the cell. 'I want him to know why he's dyin'. Reckon I can fix it so's he takes a week doin' it, same as Job.'

'He'll slow us down,' Cord objected.

'An' she won't?' Brodie growled, darting a malevolent look at Cassie. 'You plannin' to ride double?'

'There's no need.' She scurried past them all to the door. 'The deputy keeps a horse in the stable out back. Mine's there too. Come on, I'll show you.'

'Hold on.' Brodie dropped Warrinder and stared round at the office, opening the drawers of the desk, then a chest that stood against the wall. He gave a short bark of laughter, turning round holding manacles linked by a short chain. 'Look what I found. Job woulda liked this.' He fastened the fetters to Warrinder's wrists and tucked the key into his pocket, smirking at Cassie. 'You figure he's bin hopin' to die? He'll be beggin' for it by the time I'm done.'

★ ★ ★

The five horses went slowly down the hill, with no sound to mark their passing but the muffled beat of hoofs on the dirt road and the occasional jingle of a spur. They turned into Ford Street, picking up speed as they left the main cluster of buildings behind.

No life stirred in the quiet streets. Redemption was a respectable place these days and the saloons were closed by two in the morning, unless there was something special to celebrate. It had taken Jeff Warrinder three years to tame the town, three years that had ended with the killing of Job Brodie and his gang.

Folk didn't care to recall that day. Four of Redemption's citizens had died after the raid on the bank. Nobody spoke either of the final bloody showdown out on the Burville trail, and a year later they'd almost forgotten the man who'd brought them peace at such a cost, the man being taken out of town lying senseless and shackled across the back of Abe Bozeman's horse.

As they rode into the river at the crossing, Cassie held back, keeping her black mare upstream a little. In front of her was Brodie, holding the rein of the horse that carried Jeff Warrinder. Her heart was racing; the outlaws hadn't bothered to tie their prisoner to the saddle and that gave both of them a chance, but she was afraid she might kill the man instead of saving his life.

As Cassie approached the middle of

the river she suddenly heaved on the bit in the mare's mouth and slammed her heels into its sides. The horse squealed its displeasure. It plunged through the water, spraying white foam as it crashed against the horse Brodie was leading. They fell together, a flurry of hoofs passing perilously close to Warrinder's senseless body as the animals tried to regain their feet.

Tossed into the fast flowing water Cassie clung to her horse's saddle, staring wildly around for Warrinder when her head broke the surface, getting a glimpse of a pale face as she went under again. Before the water closed over her head for a second time she thought she heard the men behind her cursing, then there was no sound but the rush of water in her ears. Coming up for air some distance downstream she saw Warrinder only as a darker shadow on the water. He was face down and drifting away from her.

The black mare was swimming, and Cassie still had the reins in her hand.

She pulled the animal around to face downstream with fingers fast going numb; the river was ice cold. The sound of churning water became a roar; the treacherous stretch of river known as the Domino Rapids was just ahead, the surface a chaotic kaleidoscope of black rocks and white water. A cascade thundered through the narrow central channel, while on either side water bounced off half-submerged boulders in a wild tumult of spray.

By some miracle, Warrinder's body was swept up against the black mare. Cassie flung out a hand and took a grip on his arm. With a strength born of desperation she dragged the unconscious man's hands towards her and hitched the manacles over the saddle horn. Thus linked they raced through smooth black water, funnelled between the treacherous rocks by the force of the current.

Cassie screamed as she caught the briefest glimpse of the drop below, then she was flung against the mare's neck, tumbling over and over, water driving into her ears and nose and mouth. Her head was full of sound, she felt crushed by it, dizzy and bewildered. Something struck her thigh, then her back was pounded as if somebody had punched her, and still she was being whirled around, and there was only the black water pressing down on her, giving her no chance to breathe.

Cassie never knew whether the ordeal really ended so quickly, or whether she'd passed out for a moment. Suddenly she was floating in quiet water, choking, kicking with her feet and staring up at the sky as she gulped down air in frantic gasps. Her hand hurt; the horse's rein was wrapped around it so tight it had cut into the flesh. The black mare was still swimming, dragging Cassie towards the half-seen shallows on the eastern bank.

The cold water had eventually achieved what Brodie's attack had failed to do; Jeff Warrinder was moving his legs, staying afloat beside the mare.

Cassie grabbed a handful of mane and let herself be pulled along until she felt her legs scraping over stones, then she stumbled to her feet and up out of the river.

They were on a narrow shelf of gravel that ran down from the eastern bank. In front of them the first grey light of dawn was showing in the sky. The mare stood splay legged to keep herself upright, with Jeff Warrinder's weight hanging from the saddle. Cassie sank to her knees, trying to release herself from the tangled reins with frozen fingers, her whole body shivering violently.

Once she was free she turned her attention to Warrinder. He seemed to have lost consciousness again, but as she attempted to lift one of his arms and free the manacles from the saddlebow his eyes opened.

'Sarah?' He sounded puzzled, peering at her in the near-dark. With a great heave she lifted his hand and released him. He sagged against her and they fell to the ground, her body beneath his.

Warrinder's lips parted in a drunken grin and he lowered his mouth to hers. Cassie Hanson thrust him away with a sound of disgust and he grunted as he rolled off her, lids drifting shut over bloodshot eyes.

★ ★ ★

Since his wife died Jeff Warrinder had learnt what too much rot gut whiskey did to a man's insides, and to his head. That didn't stop him drinking. The booze-sodden oblivion only lasted a short time, and it came dear, but it was better than nothing. A clear head was the last thing a man needed when he woke every day to a world that was empty, a world where the warmth of the sun couldn't touch him. When he was sober every passing hour felt like a lifetime.

He should have died. It should have been him they buried alongside Sarah. Instead they'd laid Steve Hanson and old Mr Borovsky from the bank to rest in the cemetery at the base of the bluff. A couple of days later there'd been another ceremony when little Rosa Jennings died, giving up the struggle against the damage done by a stray bullet that had lodged in her skull. She'd been a few days short of four years old.

The bank robbers had been shovelled into a single unmarked grave a couple of miles out of town, and within a year nobody could be quite sure where they lay, but the scars they left behind in the little town weren't so easy to remove. Jeff Warrinder wasn't the only one whose life was shattered into ruin the day three men brought their deadly havoc to Redemption. But he was the only one who blamed himself for what happened, and he was the one person he could never forgive.

Jeff Warrinder groaned and tried to place his hands on his aching head. The shock when his arms refused to obey his command was enough to jolt his eyes open, but as the bright sunlight smote at him he quickly closed them again. His bone-dry mouth had been stuffed with some vile-tasting object that made him want to gag. It took a little time to realize it was his tongue.

He made a second attempt at opening his eyes, more cautiously this time. The sun was shining through leaves above his head. Despite that he was cold to the bone, his whole body shivering. He was soaking wet. Very slowly he rolled over. There was definitely something wrong with his arms. Hoisting onto his elbows and looking down he saw what it was; his wrists were decorated with a set of shackles, very much like the ones he'd kept in his office when he was Sheriff of Redemption. But that had been a lifetime ago.

A dozen aches and pains awoke as he did. Warrinder groaned again. The aftermath of his drinking bout was surely enough punishment; whatever he'd done he didn't think he deserved to be cold and wet and battered as well.

A shadow moved across him. He turned his throbbing head and saw a pair of worn moccasins.

'I bet you feel worse than dog shit.' The voice was deep and distinctive, but not one he immediately recognized. Jeff made an attempt at an answer, a string of curses coming readily to his mind, but no sound escaped from his throat. The man laughed. 'Want a drink?'

'Whiskey,' Jeff croaked. The shadow went away and he winced as the sun's brightness invaded his eyes again. A moment later the man was back. He hauled Jeff to a sitting position.

'Here.' A cup was held to his lips, metallic and warm, but the water it held tasted like salvation and Jeff drunk it down to the last drop.

'More,' he said. 'Please,' he added, when the man didn't move.

Squinting, he was able to study the stranger's features. The broad face was the colour of autumn beech leaves, lined by a great many summers. Grey hair hung in a straggly braid over each shoulder, and there was a hint of amusement in the black eyes that stared back into his. Jeff had a feeling he'd seen the man before.

'So, he finally woke up.' The voice came from behind Jeff's back. Startled to hear a woman, he tried to turn, but the effort set the drums pounding even harder in his head and he screwed his eyes shut in the hope they could be silenced.

She laughed, but it wasn't a pleasant sound. 'Asking for water, Tree. That must be a first.'

In some corner of his fuddled mind the name and the face came together and told him who these two people were. Tree Falling Smithers was a half-breed who'd once worked for young Steve Hanson; it was reasonable to assume he now worked for Steve's widow.

'Mrs Hanson?' Jeff hazarded. His mouth felt nearly as bad as it had before the water arrived. He fought the desire to vomit and stared again at the metal bracelets he wore, trying to work out how they came to be there.

'Be obliged for some more water. Real obliged. If you please,' he croaked, too desperate to let pride stand in his way. Tree came back with the cup refilled. After a long deep draught Jeff felt as if his tongue had shrunk back to something like its normal size, though it still tasted like scrapings off Pusey's floor.

'Thanks.' Jeff made a slight movement with his hand so the fetters jangled, wincing as the sound and the motion echoed through his head. 'You want to tell me what this is all about? Guess I missed something.'

'You certainly did.' Cassie Hanson's voice was light, almost musical. Jeff stared as she moved round from behind his back and hunkered down before him. There was a fresh red bruise on her forehead. 'You recall anything at all about last night?'

'I'd guess I was at Pusey's,' he said uncertainly.

'You don't remember having a fight with Rupe Krantz? Or trying to knock out Nate Grundy? Or being in jail?'

'Can't say I do. You saying Nate put these on me?' He gestured at the manacles, beginning to feel riled. He didn't remember a thing, but the sheriff had never treated him that way before.

'No. That was a man called Brodie. He wasn't too happy with you. His brother was the man you shot after the bank raid last year.'

'Brodie? It was Job Brodie's brother did this?' Jeff tried to make sense of it but failed.

Cassie sighed. 'I'll explain later. Help him into the buggy, Tree. And you'd better wrap that blanket round him, he's shivering. Lord knows I'm still frozen half to death myself; you'd think that ride would have warmed me, not to mention a dry set of clothes. Come on Mr Warrinder, I didn't save you from Brodie and the river just so you could catch your death from pneumonia.'

As the buggy jolted up from the

riverbank and on to the road Jeff decided that after all he didn't much care where he was or how he'd got there. He wasn't feeling well enough to get angry. Not yet.

4

Jeff Warrinder squatted in the shade of the veranda at the Lazy Zee, drinking his second cup of coffee and squinting across at Cassie Hanson. She sat in a rocking chair by the door to the ranch house. The clothes she wore, a man's shirt and pants tied around the middle with twine, were several sizes too big for her, and she had an old soft hat pulled low over her eyes. Even dressed that way she was still quite a woman, he decided, small in stature but real handsome.

'Feeling better?' As she spoke she lifted her head to look at him. Her green eyes made him feel uncomfortable, as if there was a bad memory half drowned in the whiskey whirlpool in his head.

'Some.' He stared into his cup and drank the coffee while it was hot enough to scald. The headache backed off a few more inches. 'You ready to tell me what happened yesterday?'

'I don't know it all. I heard you picked a fight with Rupe Krantz, which I believe you won. Then you tried to lay out Nate Grundy. Since you were too drunk to stand it wasn't much of a contest. After you threw up on the floor of his office and passed out, the sheriff locked you in the cells.'

He gave a death's head grin. 'Sounds like a fairly normal night.'

'Yes.' She gave him a sidelong glance. 'Only last night you weren't the only one in jail.'

Jeff Warrinder nodded and winced. 'A day or two back I recall Nate telling me he had a prisoner. The man who shot the driver on the Persephone stage last month made the mistake of whooping it up in the Queen of Hearts. Nate was expecting the marshals from Burville to come fetch him. I don't recollect the man's name.'

'Ross Cord,' she said. 'Only he didn't

wait around for the marshals: some of his friends came instead.' Her voice faltered. 'They killed Abe Bozeman. The one called Brodie would have killed you too once he heard your name, only you wouldn't wake up. Stabbing a man in his sleep was no fun; he wanted you to have the kind of send-off you gave his brother.'

He looked at her questioningly.

'Slow and painful,' she said.

'That's the way my mind's working.' Then he frowned suddenly, trying to rub the cobwebs from his forehead with a thumb. 'Abe? You say he's dead?'

'Brodie cut his throat.' She sounded as if she didn't care, though the truth was there to read in her green eyes and the quick nervous swallow before she went on, 'Never saw so much blood in my life.'

He saw through her matter-of-fact tone, understanding her horror. And he'd been there, too drunk to be aware of what was going on. He dropped his gaze. 'I'm sorry.'

She shrugged. 'All you did was get drunk. Like you said, a normal night.'

There was a long silence before he spoke again. 'What were you doing at the jail anyhow?'

'You and I were sharing a cell.' She half smiled at his shocked reaction. 'Bull Krantz caught me helping myself to some of his steers. Not so many as he stole from me when he was branding mavericks, but it seems that's allowed. Or it is when you're the biggest rancher in the territory.' Cassie couldn't keep the bitterness from her voice.

'Bull always played by his own rules.'

'He didn't steal from the Lazy Zee when Steve was alive. Anyway, I told Cord I was afraid I'd be standing trial for rustling, and I showed him where to find Abe's horse. When we reached the river I pretended to get in trouble where the water gets deep, so I could knock you off your horse. It was lucky the current was running fast; they weren't fool enough to come after us.'

'Brodie wanted to kill me.' He spoke in a flat toneless voice. 'And you pushed me in the river while I was blind drunk. That's twice I should have died.'

She said nothing, and Warrinder sat silent a long time. 'Guess you thought you were doing me a favour,' he said at last, sounding resigned.

Cassie shook her head. 'No. I had something else in mind. Like it or not, whether you wanted it or not, I saved your life. You owe me.'

He laughed bitterly. 'I don't own a thing in the world except what you see right here. The cabin, my horse, even my guns are gone. I drank it all.'

'What I see is good enough. You can work off your debt. Tree's fine with horses, and when he feels like it he's a fair hand with cattle, but he's no good at fixing things. My barn roof's more holes than wood.'

'I'm not a carpenter,' Jeff said.

It was Cassie's turn to laugh. 'You're a no-good drunken bum, but you're the best I can get so you'll have to do.' She rose to her feet. 'I suppose we'd better take that chain off you, but first you have to promise you won't try to leave till your debt's paid.'

'Hold on.' He rose too, eyes narrowing. 'Nate Grundy must've gone after Cord and Brodie.'

She nodded. 'I imagine so. There was another man with Brodie, I think they called him Mac.'

'Three of them. That's even worse. Nate's likely to get himself killed. He'll need help.'

Cassie Hanson snorted, a most unladylike noise. 'Just what good do you think you'd be? You just told me you've got no gun and no horse, not to mention having a hangover that's fit to beat the band. Forget it, Mr Warrinder. I'm going to fetch my Bible. Once you've sworn to give me seven days' solid work I'll have Tree cut those things off your wrists.'

'What happened to the key?'

'It's in Brodie's pocket. You want to go and ask him for it?' With that she turned on her heels and vanished into the house.

★ ★ ★

The sun was high. Jeff Warrinder balanced on the ladder and wiped sweat from his face, cursing the shackles. Removing them hadn't proved to be so easy; Tree had vanished. According to Cassie Hanson it happened often. The old half-breed went hunting or fishing, or just disappeared for a few hours without explanation. Jeff had tried to cut the chain with a chisel, but his movement was too restricted to get in a solid blow with the hammer.

Obedient to her wishes he'd sworn to give Steve Hanson's widow her seven days of labour. He'd made a start on fixing the barn roof, fighting the nausea left behind by Pusey's rot-gut whiskey and doing his best to ignore his body's craving for more.

Jeff eased back down the ladder to fetch a fresh supply of shingles, going first to the well to draw water and drinking deep. He filled the dipper from the bucket again and let his legs fold beneath him, sitting down so the stones sheltered him from the heat.

'You want something to eat?' She came to the front of the veranda, where the sunlight caught her hair and turned it into a golden halo.

The suggestion was enough to sicken him. 'Not right now, thanks.' He tipped the dipper, brought it to his mouth and emptied it once more. 'When do you think Tree will come back?'

She shrugged. 'He's usually here for his meals. Looks like you'll have one side of the roof finished by nightfall.'

'Nothing I'd rather do,' he said drily, thoughtfully licking lips that were already parched again.

'If you're thinking about a drink you can forget it; there's not a drop of liquor on the place. Anyway a few days without Pusey's firewater won't do you any harm.'

'You'd know about that, huh?'

She flushed. 'Mister, I've seen it all. My pa drank himself to death. When it comes to boozing you're nothing but a greenhorn. I'll tell you this for nothing: you want to die there's a whole lot of easier ways.' She turned her back on him then and returned to the house.

Jeff paused in his work when the rider appeared. He watched the big chestnut horse lope between the Lazy Zee's drunken gateposts.

There was no mistaking Rupe Krantz; like his father he needed a horse that could carry weight. Rupe appeared not to notice Jeff on the roof of the barn, riding straight past him and up to the ranch house. He stepped down without waiting to be asked, throwing the chestnut's rein over the hitching rail.

'Cassie? You in there?' He had his hand on the door when she pushed it open from inside. The woman drove him back on to the veranda with the empty bucket she held between her two hands.

'You've got no business here, Rupe,'

she said. 'Specially since your father had me locked up in jail.'

He laughed. 'Yeah, he told me about that. And then you broke out. That won't sound too good when the case comes to court. Lucky for you the sheriff's off looking for the men who killed his deputy. We've got time to sort things out before he gets back. You don't want any more trouble.'

She stood her ground, her eyes blazing. 'Any trouble I've got is thanks to you and your father.'

'We're always ready to be neighbourly. You and me, we ought to be friends.' Rupe was tall and powerfully built, towering over her, but he didn't have Bull's overhanging brow and stubborn down-turned mouth; the son was a pale copy of the hard-bitten old cattleman. Right now the heir to the Double Bar K didn't look his best; his left eye was swollen half-shut and his top lip was twice its normal size, dark with scabs.

'You think so?' Cassie Hanson's lips

curved in a smile, though it didn't reach her eyes. 'What happened to you, Rupe? Been wrestling with a grizzly bear?'

He ignored the taunt, moving closer, a hand reaching to touch her hair. 'I always liked you. It doesn't have to be this way between the Double Bar K and the Lazy Zee. There's something I gotta say — '

'There's nothing I want to hear,' she interrupted quickly, stepping past him and hurrying down the steps. 'Get off my land, Rupe Krantz. If you want to be a good neighbour then pay for those mavericks you stole. You know I can't afford to lose twenty head, let alone a hundred or more.'

'Reckon I can fix that. Like I said, all you have to do is be friends. I hate to see you struggling alone this way. This isn't just about being neighbours.' He followed her across the yard to the well, taking the bucket from her hand and drawing the water for her.

'It's good land you've got here, but it's going to waste with only that no-good half-breed helping out. We need to talk, you and me. It's nearly a year since Steve died. You can't run this ranch on your own, Cassie. We both of us know what you need.'

She stood back to watch as he hefted the full bucket out of the well.

'I don't recall giving you permission to make free with my name.'

'Don't you go all coy on me.' Rupe put the bucket down and reached for her, his big hand grasping her shoulder. 'Two ranches, our land right up against yours, we should be real cosy. It makes sense, Cassie,' he said. 'Bet you miss having a man around here.'

She shook her head. 'I miss Steve. That's different. Let me go, Rupe.'

He tightened his grip, pulling her closer. 'You gotta listen!'

'No she don't.' Jeff Warrinder's long hard fingers closed on the man's forearm. 'Mrs Hanson, ma'am, do you want Mr Krantz to leave?'

'Yes.' She pulled free and stood massaging her shoulder as if it hurt her.

'Please see him off my property, Mr Warrinder.'

'Mr Warrinder!' Rupe Krantz sneered. 'This drunken souse is nothing but a washed-up loser who hangs around in saloons bumming drinks.'

'You've had your say,' Jeff said. 'It's time to leave.'

Krantz gave a sidelong glance at the woman. 'Trouble is the suckers he used to call friends are tired of him; they cross the street when they see him coming.'

Jeff took a long hard look at the damage he'd inflicted on Rupe's face a couple of nights before. He grinned. 'Sure wish I could remember hitting you,' he said sorrowfully. 'Looks like I made quite a job of it.'

'You're the one who was dragged off to jail close to senseless,' Krantz shot back. He stared down at the metal bracelets on Jeff's wrists and laughed. 'And it looks like the sheriff finally got sick of you like the rest of us. Wouldn't be a fair fight while you're wearing those, but you can try me for size again soon as you like.'

'No time like right now.'

Rupe Krantz nodded. 'Fine.'

Jeff took a swift step back as a fist shot out to graze his chin. He laughed as Rupe almost lost his balance. The big man straightened, glaring at Jeff, who bounced away on his toes.

'Have to do better than that,' Jeff taunted him.

With a roar Rupe charged. In that instant Jeff got a glimpse of the bull-like rage that had made old man Krantz feared throughout the county. He tried to stand his ground but the attack drove him halfway across the yard. They went down together, Rupe grappling for a hold on Jeff's neck, Jeff sweeping the questing fingers aside before they could get a grip. Then Jeff brought his two fists swiftly back to deliver a short-armed jab to Rupe's face, scoring a hit on the swollen flesh below his left eye.

Rupe yelped. Giving up his attempt to get a stranglehold he heaved himself up. Jeff read his intention in his eyes. Hampered by the fetters, Jeff was breathing hard as he frantically scudded away on feet and elbows. It was a near run thing. Rupe dropped, but Jeff took the massive weight on his legs instead of his belly. Grasping the short length of chain in his two hands Jeff swung hard at the side of Rupe's head, making contact above his ear. Rupe grunted, but he wasn't anywhere near finished. He rolled clear before Jeff could get in another blow, coming swiftly upright.

With his hands restricted, Jeff's only hope lay in speed. He too rose to his feet, skittering backwards, trying to earn a breathing space. His head was throbbing. Rupe came rushing in, bending low to scoop up dirt with his fingers, flinging it at Jeff's face. Diving aside Jeff dodged, choking and blinking as the dust caught him. Half blinded he didn't see the bucket of water Rupe had left by the well. He crashed to the ground with the bucket tangled between his legs, his fettered arms making it impossible to cushion the fall.

Jeff landed face down. This time there was no escape. Roaring with triumph Rupe flung himself on to his victim, his great bulk slamming down and shutting out the light.

5

Rupe's weight crashed on to him and Jeff heard a bone crack, feeling the breath driven from his body.

Rupe lifted Jeff's head between huge hands. For a second there was light and his crushed ribs rose to draw in a little air, but the relief was short-lived; his face was smashed back to the ground and crushed into the dirt. Dust scoured Jeff's eyes and filled his mouth where it mixed with blood oozing down inside his nose, threatening to choke him. His lungs heaved desperately. The world was turning dark with pain, his chest a ball of fire.

Beneath him the fetters on his wrists dug into his flesh. In the split second before he passed out his mind began to work again, slow and simple, the way it did when he was on a drunk; there was something he could do. His hands were chained together but he still had the use of them. All he had to do was push hard enough and he'd lift Rupe's weight off his back. Then he could take a breath.

Jeff heaved up with every scrap of his remaining strength, his tortured lungs gulped down their fill of dusty air. He resisted the temptation to choke and jerked his head back, feeling his skull make contact with something that yielded under the blow. Rupe cursed and his hold loosened. Jeff went up sharp and sudden like a bucking horse, then dropped his left shoulder and thrust up with the right.

Unable to hold on, Rupe slid off him and the crushing weight was gone. Jeff shook himself free, rolling over and over with the clatter of the bucket ringing in his head; the handle was caught on the heel of his boot. He kept his eyes shut tight against the swirling dust until he was halfway to his feet, a sharp nudge resonating from his chest to his back reminding him of the damage Rupe had done; he'd been lucky, that crack had been no more than a couple of ribs.

Jeff kicked the bucket from him and stood up. The blood oozing into his mouth was warm and metallic. It was the first thing to chase out the taste of stale whiskey since he'd arrived at the Lazy Zee. Despite the precariousness of his position he smiled.

A few paces across the yard Rupe was getting to his feet; he saw the smile and snarled. His face too was smeared with blood and there was a fresh cut on his forehead, but with barely a pause he was barrelling back into the fight, head down in another furious bull-like rush. Jeff watched him come, turning the fetters on his wrists so he could wrap the short length of chain over his knuckles. Judging the moment to the split second he stepped aside, landing a hefty blow on Rupe's skull as the man plunged past him, just above his ear.

When he rose to his feet this time Rupe was swaying, and breathing hard, but he still kept coming, his shuffling feet carrying him relentlessly to the attack. Jeff revised his opinion of the man; if bloody-minded determination counted for anything, he looked set to inherit his father's nickname.

'Haven't you had enough?' Jeff asked, stepping back to put some distance between them. He smeared the back of his hand across his face, spreading blood into his tangled beard.

'You wish,' Rupe snarled. 'I've barely started, *Mister* Warrinder.'

They came together again. This time Rupe anticipated Jeff's side-step, and they clashed head on like a pair of rutting bucks. As before Rupe's weight gave him the advantage, and he lifted Jeff off his feet in a wrestling hold, powerful arms linking so his huge fists were crushing against his enemy's spine.

Rupe's face was only inches away, battered and bloody but showing no sign of weakness; he gave Jeff an evil grin and began to squeeze.

This time Jeff had used his head. As Rupe stormed in he'd lifted his arms, deliberately letting the man in under his defence. Now he brought the chain of the fetters down between their two bloody and contorted faces, pressing it hard against Rupe's throat. He straightened his arms, bearing away, his muscles taut with strain.

Jeff's back was slowly bending in ways it wasn't meant to go. Another half-inch and surely it would give way. He leant doggedly on the fetters, the metal bracelets biting into his wrists. Rupe's face was turning purple as the chain dug deep in to his neck. He choked, his teeth bared in an angry snarl.

It was Rupe who gave way, barely able to stay upright, his lungs so starved of air that his swollen lips were turning blue. Jeff broke free and stood splayfooted, amazed that his aching back was still whole, warily watching his huge opponent as he sagged against the well. Rupe leant on the coping, gasping for breath, his hands exploring the damage to his neck where the metal links had left dark marks.

Tree had reappeared. He stood by the ranch-house steps close to Cassie Hanson, silent and watchful, an ancient rifle held loosely in one hand. Rupe Krantz started shakily towards the rail where he'd hitched his horse. The half-breed spat expressively, but at a word from the woman he untied the chestnut's reins and stepped forward to hand them to the defeated man.

Rupe heaved himself into the saddle, moving slow as if the effort pained him. He glared down at Jeff Warrinder. 'This isn't finished,' he said hoarsely, then he shifted his gaze to Cassie.

'You're damaged goods, lady. You'll regret taking sides with that washed-up drunk. No decent woman chooses a man like him.' With that he gave a savage jerk on the reins to pull the horse's head around.

The soft thud of hoofbeats receded. Krantz left a long silence behind him. Cassie Hanson retreated into the house, slamming the door. Jeff fingered his nose and was surprised to find it wasn't broken.

Tree fetched the water bucket, filled it and brought it to Jeff. He plunged his head in, along with his raw and bleeding knuckles, and came up spluttering, shaking himself so water flew from his unkempt hair and beard. He staggered just a little, then he straightened. 'If you've got no objection,' he said, holding out his manacled hands, 'I'd be obliged if you'd get these things off me.'

The lines on Tree's face deepened as a slight smile chased over his features, then he was solemn again. 'Good weapon,' he commented, but he headed for the back of the barn where the tools were kept.

★　★　★

'C'mon, Eli, what d'you reckon?' Nate Grundy curbed his horse impatiently, staring at the marks peppering the river's edge. Cord and his gang would

70

be miles ahead. The sun was already climbing up the sky; he'd wasted too much time getting the posse organized.

Eli Ranovich shook his head silently and urged his bony grey into the stream. When he reached the shallows near the other bank he pulled up and climbed stiffly out of the saddle, landing in a couple of inches of water. He bent low, his face only inches from the gravelly shore. 'Makes no sense,' he said at last. 'Purty sure five horses went in, but I can't make it more'n four comin' out.'

'Maybe they lost a horse. Which means they could be ridin' double,' Jim Ormond suggested.

'Could be they brought Jeff Warrinder this far and no further,' Nate Grundy countered. 'When a man's got that much drink in him he'd drown without even stirring in his sleep.'

'If they tipped him into the river that don't explain why there's one horse less,' Eli said.

'You really think they took Jeff and

71

Mrs Hanson along?' Ormond asked. 'Why risk being slowed up?'

'Cord wasn't alone when he robbed that stage, and he didn't let himself out of jail,' Grundy said. 'I've been thinking about who came to fetch him, and I've come up with the name of Jeremiah Brodie.'

Jim Ormond looked at him blankly. 'That supposed to mean something?'

'Only that you got a short memory, Jim. Must be the noise from that hammer of yours, or maybe the heat of the fire. Brodie's brother Job was one of the men Jeff killed a year ago, when his Sarah died.'

'That don't account for Cassie Hanson. Steve was shot too, but that don't give 'em no call to kidnap his widow.'

Old Eli snorted. 'Use your head. She's a purty woman, an' she's just seen Abe get his throat cut. You figure they'd leave her behind? Tell you this for sure: with the river runnin' fast there ain't much chance for a man to get out of the water once he drifted down from the crossin', he'd go over the Domino and hit them rocks by Parry's pool.' He led the grey to a fallen tree and stepped up on it so he could heave himself back into the saddle. 'Nothin' more to see here.'

'Then let's make tracks.' The sheriff spurred out of the water, the rest of the posse following. 'They'll be heading for the high country.'

'I know you didn't want me along, Nate.' Eli Ranovich brought his bony old grey alongside the sheriff's horse. 'I won't deny that at my age the thought of sittin' on my own back porch looks a helluva lot more temptin' than chasin' a bunch of killers into the mountains. Thought I'd done with all this when Jeff made you his deputy.'

Nate Grundy turned uneasy eyes on the old man. 'I'm sorry, Eli. You and Abe were Redemption's oldest citizens, wouldn't do to lose the both of you in one week.'

Eli snorted. 'You think I'm gonna fall

off my horse an' break my neck? If the pace gets too much for me I'll holler.' He looked round at the four men riding a little way behind and lowered his voice. 'Fact is, Nate, you need me. Not another man here who's ridden on a posse, and it don't promise to be no picnic.'

'I know it. But for Cord and his buddies taking off with Jeff and Mrs Hanson I'd have waited for more help,' Grundy said, 'but we need to catch them before they get holed up in the hills. Sure wish those marshals from Burville were here.'

He didn't even know how many men they were chasing. Suppose both Jeff and Mrs Hanson had died at the river crossing, the one killed out of vengeance, the other because she'd seen a man commit murder? There could be four outlaws ahead of them, and that made for pretty poor odds.

Besides Eli, and Jim, who was Redemption's blacksmith, he'd deputized Louis Jardine from the stockyard.

Louis was a reliable man, but not exactly skilled with a gun. That left the two young cowboys who'd just quit working for Bull Krantz; they'd only signed on because they'd lost their shirts in a poker game and needed a stake to get them out of town.

✓ Eli eased his horse to a jog as they crossed a patch of loose sand, his eyes scanning the scuff marks in the dirt. 'I'd still swear we're only followin' four horses, and one of 'em don't look to be carryin' a load. But I guess Mrs Hanson don't weigh heavy. Or it could be they had a mount along for Cord, and decided to steal Abe's horse as a spare.'

The sheriff didn't reply, staring at the ground, unable to read the signs the old man saw so plain. It was a skill he needed to learn. His mouth drew into a tight line; if one rider had been abandoned at the river he had a fair idea who it was. Jeff Warrinder might have turned into a drunken wreck after his wife died, but that didn't change the debt owed him by the town of Redemption. Besides, he'd been a friend.

As the day ended with a blaze of red to the west they were still fifteen miles or more from the mountains.

'Hey, Sheriff, I figure that's a dust cloud.' Bronc, one of the young cowboys, spurred his horse alongside Grundy. 'Look, see where the light's catchin' it.'

'Could be,' the sheriff said. 'Still puts us a powerful long way behind. We'll ride till full dark, rest up a few hours then go on once the moon's high enough to see by.'

With a groan, Eli Ranovich eased his weight in the saddle. 'Don't reckon I could get off this damn cayuse if I tried.'

Monty, Bronc's partner, rode up to join them as the horses picked up speed. 'Sheriff, there's somethin' we didn't tell you. That gal, the one you reckon they've taken with 'em.'

'Cassie Hanson? What about her?'

'See, me an' Bronc feel bad about her bein' out there. We was ridin' with the boss when he caught her with them steers. That deputy, the one they killed, he wasn't none too keen on lockin' up a woman. If'n we hadn't backed Mr Krantz, I don't reckon she would've been in jail.'

'Are you saying it wasn't true? Didn't you find Mrs Hanson with a bunch of Bull's cattle?'

'Well, yeah.' Monty looked uncomfortable. 'But that weren't nothin' compared to all them mavericks we helped run off her land a few months back. Sure, every rancher feels he's free to take the odd cleanskin that wanders onto his range, seems like the fella who owns 'em deserves what he gets if he ain't doin' his job right, but we must've put the Double Bar K brand on well nigh a hundred hides where it didn't belong.'

'She didn't have much to show for that year's breedin',' Bronc agreed. 'It's tough on a woman, tryin' to run a spread on her own, reckon it was bad enough her husband gettin' killed by them bank robbers. And now it looks like Mr Krantz is all-fired set on puttin' her out of business.'

'Wasn't that way to start,' Monty said. 'I recall the month after the shootin', Rupe an' his old man rode over to the Lazy Zee to ask if'n she needed any help. They was real friendly. Me an' a couple more cowboys spent a week fixin' her fences an' diggin' out a fresh water-hole. Fact is, that's why we come an' joined up with this here posse. She's a real nice little lady. Sure do hope we can find her, put things right some.'

'Amen to that,' Grundy said, buttoning his lip on the thought that the young widow would be a good catch for a down-at-heel cowhand. He squinted at the sky. Bronc and Monty would back him all the way, along with the rest of the posse; they'd all do their best to bring Cassie Hanson back alive and unharmed, but the light was almost gone. It would take a lot more than six men to run the outlaws down once they reached the canyons.

6

Two full days had passed since the fight with Rupe Krantz. Jeff Warrinder groaned as he rolled out of his blankets onto the floor of the barn at the Lazy Zee. He was dog tired; he should have slept like the dead, but instead he'd tossed and turned through the hours of darkness in the stall next to Cassie Hanson's black mare. When he eventually closed his eyes his sleep was troubled with nightmares. He'd wake with his head full of disturbing visions that were slow to leave him, even when the sun rose.

He pulled on his boots, doing his best to ignore the slight tremor in his hands. The repairs to the barn would be finished in a few hours. He had no idea what else Mrs Hanson had in mind for him to do; she hadn't spoken to him since Rupe rode away. If they met she avoided his eyes; Jeff had begun to feel invisible.

As always Tree brought him coffee and breakfast. Only this time the old man silently handed Jeff a razor and towel. Jeff stared at the half-breed critically; Tree had inherited a lot of characteristics from his mother's race, including a lack of facial hair. 'These aren't yours,' Jeff said.

Tree jerked his head expressively towards the house. Trust a woman to want to start changing a man, even if she'd only got hold of him for a few days. Jeff fingered his tangled beard, still matted in places with dried blood.

'What did she say?'

The dark eyes studied him for a moment. 'She say, I should teach you to braid your hair.'

Despite himself Jeff grinned. It was just the kind of remark Sarah might have come up with. 'Go back and tell her I'd prefer to have it cut. Reckon that's woman's work, seeing as she won't want me taking time off to go to the barber shop, not to mention I don't have ten cents to my name.'

A while later, clean shaven but with his hair still hanging loose to his shoulders, Jeff was putting the last patch on the barn roof. The cracked ribs and the bruises from Rupe's rough handling were very much with him, and climbing up and down a ladder was hard on a man's knees, but most of the aches and pains eased as his muscles warmed up. If it wasn't for the relentless thirst that was tightening its hold on him with each passing hour Jeff thought he'd have been feeling pretty good.

The need for a drink burnt in his brain, and now and then tremors shook him. By noon he'd worked up a fair pitch of anger; some part of him knew it should have been aimed at himself, but it was easier to blame Cassie Hanson. How come he was paying her for saving a life he no longer wanted? Brodie or Cord would have finished him and he'd have known nothing about it. The damn woman never should have interfered.

Jeff was about ready to jump off the roof and walk to town by the time the approaching dust cloud told him there was a rider coming. It wasn't Tree; he'd ridden to the south range and wasn't expected back until nightfall. Hammering the last nail into place with unnecessary force Jeff slid down to the ladder and pitched the tools off the roof. He followed them so fast he almost lost his footing on the rungs. Let it be Rupe Krantz coming to try his luck again; a hard fight might drive out the demon riding his shoulder.

As the rider drew nearer Jeff grinned savagely; it had to be Rupe, there weren't many men that big. His hands had almost stopped shaking, and he flexed them hopefully into fists. The horse emerged from the plume of dust, a big animal. It wasn't Rupe's chestnut, but it was one he recognized.

Bull Krantz rode an iron-grey stallion. He curbed it hard as he came past the Lazy Zee's unhinged gate so it plunged and half reared before coming to a sliding halt outside the ranch house.

'Real pretty,' Jeff said, stepping into view from the shade of the barn, keeping his frayed temper under a rein as tight as that controlling the stallion. He had to work off the craving in his head, this fierce relentless itch that he couldn't scratch. Father or son, it made no difference; he needed a fight. 'Morning, Bull. How's Rupe?'

'He's gone to Burville for a few days.' The rancher stared down at him, craggy brow lowering over small eyes. 'What's it to you?'

Jeff's mouth curved into a grin and he fingered one of the bruises on his face, left there by his latest encounter with Rupe. 'Maybe he didn't tell you who broke his nose for him.'

'I didn't see him before he left. Might have guessed the two of you were fighting again. I'm surprised you can still afford the drink, even Pusey's rot gut costs money.'

'You know, it was more of a pleasure taking him on without it. If the boy gets hurt now and then it's all your fault, Bull; you should've taught the kid some manners.'

Bull glowered. 'What're you talking about?'

'He was upsetting Mrs Hanson, wouldn't go when she asked him to leave.'

'Since when is what Mrs Hanson wants any business of yours?' Bull stepped off his horse, leaving it ground-reined as he advanced on Jeff.

'Since I came to work here. Besides, Rupe don't have to work hard to make himself offensive; that boy of yours can get me riled just by breathing too loud. It's a talent that runs in the family.' He studied the man, measuring him up; Bull had seen the passage of nearly fifty years, but they'd only made him harder. They were so ill-matched in weight that Jeff's comparative youth would give him no advantage. 'Seems to me you won't be welcome either, seeing you had Mrs

Hanson arrested for taking back some of the cattle you stole.'

Bull ignored the insult. He turned to look at the barn roof. 'Nice job you've done; I appreciate that. I've got plans for this place.'

Jeff laughed aloud. 'So that's it! You figure on taking over here. You shouldn't have sent a boy to do a man's job, Bull. Like I said, Rupe needs to learn some manners. Reckon if I hadn't been here to throw him out Mrs Hanson would've done it herself.'

'Keep your nose out of things that don't concern you,' Bull said. 'The woman's a little slow making up her mind but she'll come around. She'd better. Nothing to stop me taking her back to jail for rustling my cattle.'

'I'd advise against it,' Jeff said.

By now they were only two yards apart. Bull swung back from his inspection of the barn to stare down into Jeff's face, his wide shoulders hunching, his square chin jutting aggressively.

'There's no badge on your vest now, Warrinder. You'd better move on.' He felt in his pocket, bringing out a silver dollar held between his finger and thumb. 'Why don't you go and buy yourself a drink? Shouldn't take you more than three hours to walk into town.'

An unholy joy ran through Jeff's veins. The craving was all but gone, driven out by the blood pounding in his temples. He grinned savagely as he stepped forward; true, he wasn't a lawman any more, but then there had been times when that badge was a curb on his freedom. Bouncing on his toes he struck the other man's hand to send the coin spinning into the air. 'Rupe's not the only one who needs a lesson in manners.'

'You think you're man enough then go ahead,' Bull roared, standing his ground, square and solid like a pillar of rock, not even bothering to lift his fists.

'Stop this.' Cassie Hanson's voice was sharp. Neither man had heard her coming, but she stood at the bottom of the ranch-house steps, her face flushed pink, her green eyes lit with an angry fire. 'I'd be obliged if you'd find some other place for your brawling. This is my home, not a downtown saloon. Mr Warrinder, you're here to work.'

'Roof's finished,' Jeff said shortly, not taking his eyes off Bull.

'Then get started on the gate. Perhaps once it's back in place people won't come riding in here without an invitation. As for you, Mr Krantz, please leave. We have nothing to say to each other. If you want to charge me with rustling I suggest you speak to the sheriff. You can tell him I'll be right here if he decides to put me under arrest.'

'Nate Grundy's still out with that posse. Word is, he's looking for you. Seems to think you took to the hills with that gang of outlaws.'

Cassie Hanson's eyes widened in surprise, then she glared at Jeff as if he was the one who'd spoken. 'The gate,' she said.

'Sure,' he replied, not taking his eyes of Bull Krantz, 'just as soon as I've seen this big-mouthed bastard go through it.'

Bull snorted. 'You think you're quite a man, Warrinder, but since they took away that badge you're nothing. Hell, you're less than nothing, hiding behind a woman's skirts while better men risk their lives riding with a posse.' He turned to Cassie.

'I gather Rupe didn't have much of a chance to talk to you the other day, but he'll be back. It doesn't make sense you trying to keep this place going, not on your own. A woman needs a man to take care of her. You don't think this bum's ready to give up the booze and stay here? First time you let him loose in town he'll end up sleeping in the gutter again — that's if the sheriff doesn't put him back in jail.'

'My decision has nothing to do with Mr Warrinder. This ranch belongs to me, and this is where I plan to stay. I don't want to see either you or your son on my land again. The pair of you are no better than thieves, and I don't care who hears me say it.'

Bull took a threatening step towards her, his big face reddening. 'Nobody calls me a thief — '

A fist struck him on the mouth, silencing him. Jeff grinned into Bull's outraged face, flung a left at the huge man's ribs then ducked away. The rancher recovered quickly, roaring with rage as he followed, powering in on his smaller opponent. Undaunted Jeff rode the first punch, his head snapping back with the force of it, getting in another hook at Bull's chin in return then retreating on nimble feet. Bull followed him, charging across the dusty ground, bellowing like his namesake.

'Stand up and fight,' the rancher demanded, as Jeff dodged his next attack. 'You're supposed to be a man, not a godamn girl!'

'Sure, if that's the way you want it.'

Jeff Warrinder barrelled in low and

fast, taking the older man around the waist, the speed of his charge overcoming the rancher's weight advantage. They crashed to the ground, both grappling for a hold.

The water, ice cold and flung with all Cassie Hanson's strength, hit them a solid blow. 'Are you deaf, or just stupid?' she screamed, dipping the bucket into the water trough for a second time. The next deluge brought both men gasping to their feet.

She pushed between them, swinging the empty bucket by the handle to drive them apart. 'Bull Krantz, you get off my land this minute or so help me I'll fetch a shotgun and put a hole in that great carcass of yours. You're nothing but an overgrown bully. If I'm going to get myself hanged it might as well be in a good cause. As for you' — she turned on Jeff, her cheeks glowing with anger — 'I'm darned if I know why I let a drunken no-hoper stay here in the first place.'

As Jeff looked down into Cassie

Hanson's flashing green eyes something inside him lurched. It hurt far worse than anything Rupe or Bull had dished out. The unhealed wound Sarah had left in his heart was suddenly split wide open. Jeff turned his back in bewilderment, heading blindly for the barn, not even waiting to see Bull Krantz ride away.

★　★　★

'This is it.' Eli straightened to look up at Nate Grundy. The posse had wasted hours following false trails that led them into blind canyons then petered out, the fear of ambush riding their shoulders at every step. At last they'd entered a great split that took them deep into the mountains, with walls of stone towering close on either side. As they turned a corner they could see a huge rock that spanned the canyon some fifty foot above the sandy floor. Eli got down from his horse stiffly and bent low to the ground to study the tracks left in the dust, advancing slowly on the great archway and stopping when he was ten yards from it.

The old man was scowling as he lifted back into his saddle. 'Four horses. They went this way quite a while ago, before dawn maybe. And they didn't come out. I shoulda known.'

'Known what? You sure this time? Why this one?' the sheriff asked.

'Because this here's Hell's Gate. Must be twenty years since I was with the posse that ran the Meacher gang to ground here; place had a bad name even then. Lost count of how often I've heard it mentioned since; can't be a badman from Vasquez to the James brothers wasn't supposed to be holed up here sometime.'

'So we don't just ride in there,' Nate Grundy said.

'Not unless you're tired of livin'.' Eli pulled his horse's head round, turning his back on the wind-sculpted gateway.

'Hold it!' Nate pushed his horse alongside him. 'You quitting?'

'That depends what you got in mind to do. I ain't ridin' into that canyon, Nate.' He gave a wintry smile, showing a scattering of teeth like crooked tombstones. 'Nothin' personal. Wouldn't even ride in there alongside Jeff Warrinder.'

'So you say we give up? What about Mrs Hanson?'

'Didn't say we give up.' Eli glanced at the sky, a narrow channel of blue high above. 'Close to noon. Maybe we should light a fire an' have ourselves some coffee, see if we can figure somethin' out.' But he wouldn't meet Nate's eyes.

Grundy hesitated, then he lit down from his horse and tossed the reins to Louis Jardine. Cautiously, hugging the thin line of shadow on the side that faced north, Nate edged into Hell's Gate. Ahead he could see the midday sun shining clear on the opposite wall, but it didn't light the trail that curved out of sight where the canyon veered further into the mountains. Here the track passed into a deep gloom, and a timeless silence. There was so little of welcome, such an abiding menace about the place, it might truly have been the entrance to the Devil's kingdom.

Nate crept forward until he was almost beyond the arch. He could make out the next twist in the trail, vanishing round a great buttress of rock that soared up through the shadows, only its very tip lit by the sun.

'Nate . . . ' Eli's voice held a plea, and, as the sheriff turned towards him, the crack of a single rifle shot rang out. A flake of stone chipped off the rock face by Nate Grundy's head and scorched past his forehead. He ducked and ran swiftly back the way he'd come. Back with the rest of the posse he put a hand to his scalp and it came away wet with blood. Behind him in the canyon the sound of the gunshot echoed, fading slowly into silence.

'Seem to recall there was water about half a mile back,' Nate said, wiping bloody fingers down his shirt and reclaiming his horse. 'Where the canyon widens out some. We'll camp there.' He glared at Eli Ranovich. 'You can tell us how you and that posse took the Meacher gang.'

'Didn't say we took 'em,' Eli muttered.

7

Nate Grundy paced between the dying fire and the horse line, back and forth under the shadow cast by a thin sliver of moon. Louis Jardine was standing guard and the rest of the posse had turned in, but Nate didn't want to sleep. He figured if he could just look at the problem long enough an answer would come to him.

Eli's story kept running through his head. Twenty years back two members of a posse had died when they tried to force their way into Hell's Gate; the rest had retreated, three of the survivors with bullet wounds. The Meacher gang had eventually been taken by a company of troopers, but not by a frontal assault. The soldiers had brought two field guns to Hell's Gate, moving them slowly forward while the soldiers sheltered behind wooden shields made from the sides of the detachment's supply wagon. They had kept up a constant barrage, day and night until the outlaws surrendered.

'Reckon Meacher's men couldn't stand the noise no longer,' Eli had said sourly. 'The canyon widens out about three hundred yards up. Place is full of caves, specially on the southern side. We rode in there later an' took a look at the one they was livin' in. Only a handful of shots even came close. Funny thing though, the two older Meachers went to the gallows without sayin' a word about what happened to their kid brother. Young Billy Meacher never was found. The soldiers figured he must have got shot an' his brothers buried him under the rocks someplace. Nobody ever knew for sure.'

Nate didn't have an army. He couldn't think of any way to break into the canyon. It would be suicide to ride through Hell's Gate; according to Eli the ground became rougher and a whole lot steeper just around that bend he'd seen, so they couldn't go in hard and fast. The young sheriff stopped when his steps carried him to the fire for the fiftieth time. He poured coffee from the battered pot. Louis Jardine came across to join him, peering at an ancient timepiece that he pulled from his vest pocket.

'Time for Bronc's watch,' Jardine said. 'Then you're next. Figure you ought to get yourself some sleep, Sheriff.'

'Can't seem to settle,' Nate replied. The thought of a decent woman like Mrs Hanson in the hands of Ross Cord and his gang was like a thorn digging ever deeper into his flesh. And there was Jeff Warrinder's death to avenge . . .

Louis Jardine shrugged and stepped over to shake Bronc. The cowboy, instantly awake in the way of his kind, leapt up with a mock salute, taking the scattergun. Jardine wrapped himself up in his bedroll and within minutes his snores mingled with those of old Eli.

Bronc came across to Nate, grinning. 'Peaceful, ain't it?' He helped himself to coffee. 'I was thinkin', Sheriff: you figure anyone ever tried to take that place from the back? See, I was lookin' at where the water comes down, along on the north wall there. Reckon there's level ground not far from what you can see. Before it got dark I walked back aways.' He nodded towards the looming heights. 'There's kind of a gully runs down, goin' across the cliff, and I reckon we could climb it. Looks like we'd be headin' in the right direction, and maybe we'd get to the top of the falls. Might be worth a look.'

'It might at that. Leastways it's something to think about.' Suddenly tired, Nate tossed the dregs of coffee onto the fire and picked up his bedroll. Staying awake wasn't going to do Mrs Hanson any good; he'd come to the problem fresh in the morning.

★   ★   ★

'Not even a damn mountain goat could climb up there,' Louis Jardine said glumly.

99

'You plan on sproutin' wings, Nate?' Jim Ormond asked, shifting his feet as he leant back against the rock and looked uneasily at the drop beneath them.

'No.' Nate Grundy followed Ormond's gaze. It was a long way down into the narrow canyon. Turning his head he stared at the sheer face above for a long moment before admitting defeat. 'Sure hope Monty and Bronc are doing better.'

Leaving Eli at the camp to mind the horses the five men had climbed up the fault that ran across the rock face, and made it to the place where the water fell in a narrow cascade to the bottom of the canyon. Then they had followed the stream, scrambling over tumbled rivers of stone and hauling themselves up slabs of rock, but they couldn't find a way to head west. At last Nate had discovered a narrow shelf that skirted the canyon halfway up, but it petered out just as the great archway over Hell's gate came into view.

The two young cowboys had gone on, still following the bed of the stream, though it was dry now, the summer trickle of water coming from a slit in the rock close to the place where they'd separated.

'We'd best get back,' Nate said heavily. 'Can't go no further this way; don't reckon a goat could make it. Take it slow, Jim, keep your eyes on Louis, he'll show you where to put your feet.'

They eased back the way they'd come, to the spot where they'd parted from Monty and Bronc. It was hot, the sun high enough to penetrate into the little gully that wound ever upwards. The cowboys' spurs lay on the rock where they'd left them; there was no sign of the two men. Nate drank a mouthful of water from the hole in the rock and filled his canteen. 'They haven't come back so maybe they made it?' he said. 'Jim, I ain't easy about leaving Eli alone this long; we'll look a lot of darned fools if Cord and his gang ride out while we're stuck up here. You reckon you can make it back down?'

'Sure.' The blacksmith looked relieved

not to be asked to climb any higher.

The sheriff slung his rifle on his back and looked at Louis Jardine, who shrugged.

'I'm with you, Nate, though I can think of a lot of things I'd rather be doin' right now.'

The climb wasn't as bad as it looked. Gradually the sky above widened out and half an hour later Nate found himself standing on a bare ridge of rock. He grunted with relief, rubbing at the aching muscles in his thighs; at least here a man could stand on his own two feet.

'Felt like a fly crawlin' up a crack in a wall,' Louis Jardine said, heaving himself up to stand beside Nate.

To the west was a tall pinnacle that stood higher than the surrounding jumble of rock. 'I saw that from inside the Gate,' Nate said, nodding. 'Reckon that's where we gotta be.'

'Can't see Monty and Bronc,' Louis said.

'Ground's pretty broken, but they

can't be far. Come on.' He led the way, making the best pace he could on the rough terrain.

They worked their way gradually nearer to the rocky spire. Once Nate thought he saw movement up ahead, but in the midday haze he wasn't sure if it was a black cowboy hat or a crow skimming low above the ground. From the ridge they couldn't see into the canyon, so there was no way to judge whether they had passed Hell's Gate.

At last only a dozen yards separated them from their objective, but here an ancient upheaval had left sharp ripples of rock pointing at the sky, like the spiny armoured back of some long dead animal. As they struggled across this last obstacle the crack of a rifle shot split the silence, rapidly followed by the unmistakable sound of a scattergun, then a smattering of fire that echoed against the walls of the canyon below.

'Them boys wasn't carryin' no shotgun,' Jardine said.

With a muttered oath the sheriff set

off at a stumbling run across the broken ground, ignoring the pain as jagged blades of rock slashed his legs above his boots, drawing blood.

More shots sounded. They saw Bronc first. He lay just below the skyline under the cover of a boulder.

'Keep low,' the cowboy warned, his voice husky. The two men obeyed, bending almost double, coming breathless to the cowboy's side.

'Never figured they'd see us,' Bronc said. His tanned face was pale; he had a hand clamped over his forearm and there was blood oozing between his fingers. 'You see Monty?'

'No. Where'd he go?' Nate asked, taking a quick look at the youngster's wound. The bullet had passed right through the arm from front to back; he'd be lucky if it hadn't broken a bone on the way.

'There.' Bronc nodded towards the far side of the pinnacle. 'There's a place you can climb up a ways. Figured he'd see better down the canyon from there, but they must've got him spotted. Wasn't nobody in sight that I could see, don't even know where the shots came from. When I heard 'em I fired back, but they got me pinned down. Besides, I couldn't rightly say who I was shootin' at . . . ' He broke off and gritted his teeth as Louis tied a bandanna round his arm.

'I'll go take a look-see,' Nate said, crouching, easing his way back across the rocky spines and working around to the place Bronc had indicated. He found the young cowboy by the pinnacle. Monty wasn't ever going to be swinging a lariat again. Nate's face hardened as he stared into the grey eyes. Lips the colour of ash were drawn back into a rictus of pain, splashed at the corner with red where the man had bitten through his tongue.

A shiny red smear across the rock showed where Monty had fallen; the bullet had taken him full in the belly. A great puddle of blood oozed around him. The sickly scent of death lay heavy on the mountain top.

Nate slithered on until he could see the opposite wall of the canyon. He poked his head up cautiously. At once a rifle cracked, and splinters of rock flew from just below him, making him duck.

'Nate?' Louis Jardine sounded scared.

'Be there in a minute,' Nate called back, thinking hard. Fired from below and with the gunman at least forty yards away it had been a good shot. He'd already killed Monty and winged Bronc; looked like they had a marksman down there. Careful to stay out of sight, Nate retreated, standing up where he wouldn't be seen. He bent to gather some fragments of rock into his hand.

Flinging the stones to rattle and clatter down into the canyon on the other side of the pinnacle, Nate dived forward, moving fast. The gunmen down below snapped off several shots but they were all aimed at his diversion, smashing into the ridge to ricochet away. Before he hit the deck again Nate had got a fair view of the land below.

The way into the canyon was steep, just as Eli said. On a level patch of land at the top of the trail there were horses tethered. Beyond that the valley widened into a deep bowl, with the top hundred feet or so sheer to the ridge. The black mouth of a huge cave yawned in the opposite canyon wall, just below that unbroken rock-face.

Some of the shots might have come from inside the cave, but there were other smaller openings; it was impossible to tell where the gunmen were hidden. Short of using a rope there was no hope of getting down there, and that would be about as sensible as walking through Hell's Gate and asking the outlaws for a cup of coffee.

Nate returned to Monty, kneeling to close the staring eyes. As he reached out his hand he recoiled in amazement. The cowboy had blinked.

'Sorry, Sheriff.' The words were scarcely a whisper. 'Guess I messed up. Bronc OK?'

'Took a slug in the arm. He'll mend.'

A sound between a cough and a moan issued from the dying man. Monty was trying to laugh. One hand fluttered weakly towards the terrible wound in his belly.

'Lousy deputies you got.' He choked and a spasm of pain fleeted across the drawn features. 'Sure wish we'd been able to find that little lady . . . ' The cowboy's hand fell back to his side as a last breath rattled in his throat.

This time there was no response as Nate leant over to close the sightless eyes.

'Dammit.' Louis Jardine had crawled across to join him. 'Now what?'

'Plenty of loose rock up here, we'll make sure the coyotes don't get him. How's Bronc?'

'He got lucky; the bones ain't broke. Won't be easy gettin' him across these rocks an' down that damn cliff though.'

A while later Nate Grundy stood by the heap of stones that covered Monty's body and wiped his hands down the sides of his pants. He'd been on a losing streak ever since they left Redemption; with only five of them left and one man hurt, there was nothing to do but return to town with his tail between his legs like a whipped pup. No wonder it had taken an army to scour the Meacher gang out of Hell's Gate canyon.

Nate didn't say a word as he led the way back across the razor-sharp rock. His thoughts were bitter. He could try and raise another posse, but it would take time; if Cassie Hanson was in the hands of Cord and his cronies she might be better off dead.

8

Jeff Warrinder lifted a shaking hand and thrust it into his mouth, biting down hard. He was sitting with his back against the wall of the barn, staring sightlessly into the night sky, seeing neither the moon nor the scattered brightness of the stars. In all the months since Sarah's death he'd never gone this long without a drink; he could hardly believe just how tight the demon held him in its grip.

The need for whiskey drove his mind around in circles. Had Cassie Hanson told the truth when she said there was no liquor in the house? He could go take a look; he might be a drunken no-hoper like she said, but he was still man enough to deal with a woman and an old half-breed.

The back door of the ranch house opened and Tree came out, stalking silently to the ramshackle lean-to where he slept. Hinges squealed a protest as the door closed then there was silence again.

From within the barn came the soft rustle as a horse shifted its feet. Jeff thought about throwing a saddle on Cassie Hanson's black mare and riding into Redemption. If he couldn't bum a few drinks he'd have to offer Pusey his boots. Or he could find a stranger too stupid or drunk to know better, and sell him the mare.

Time passed. He went on sitting there, chewing on his hand. The light in the ranch house went out. Licking blood from skin punctured by his own teeth, Jeff rose stiffly to his feet, turning to stare into the darkness of the barn. He took a step, then another. It wouldn't take a minute to saddle the mare.

'It's a fine night.'

He whipped round. Cassie Hanson stood on the veranda. A long robe was clutched round her body, and her hair hung loose over her shoulders, silvered by the moonlight. She was beautiful. Jeff stared at her in silence.

The woman's lips curved in a mocking smile. 'Going somewhere?'

'What's that to you?' A sudden anger took him and his voice was rough.

'Three more days labour,' she replied evenly. 'I should have known you wouldn't see it through.'

'I fixed the barn and the gate. Reckon I kept my side of the bargain.'

Jeff folded his arms to hide the trembling in his hands. He stared at the calm face, pale against the darkness. What could Cassie Hanson know? Without the whiskey he had to face the guilt that tore him apart, and it was too much. He'd killed his wife, as sure as if he'd broken her neck with his own bare hands.

'Reckon you did well getting four days out of me. Never did think my life was worth much.'

'It could be,' she said, stepping off the veranda and walking towards him.

'Jeff?' She looked into his face and wordlessly reached out to him. He stared down at her hands, small and white in the moonlight, inviting him to take a hold. The fingers were calloused with hard work. Jeff's anger died. This woman was alone too; she'd lost her husband that same terrible day. Something inside him twisted and again he felt that new pain, just as he had after the fight with Bull.

'My father never had the strength to escape,' she said. 'He always let it beat him, time after time. Is that the way it's going to be with you?' Moisture shone in her eyes. 'You're not the only one who wishes things had turned out different. The day you lost your Sarah I lost Steve, and the last words I ever spoke to him were hard and mean. We'd argued over some little thing and he drove off in a temper. And he never came back. I didn't get a chance to tell him how sorry I was.'

She bit her lip. 'We can't go on blaming ourselves, Jeff. There's still a lot of life to live.'

'What if I can't do it?' he said.

She tightened her grip on his trembling fingers. 'You can,' she said. 'You got this far.' Then she was in his arms, the softness of her hair against his cheek, the generous curves of her body warming him. 'We'll get through it together.'

★ ★ ★

Nate Grundy rode a day and a half without speaking a word, driving his horse hard. His thoughts were bitter; he'd never known how good Jeff Warrinder was at his job. Redemption's former sheriff had made it look easy, even when they'd ridden back with one of their number missing or a body draped over a saddle, it hadn't felt like a waste. Not that Jeff held his men's lives lightly, but in the three years Nate had been his deputy he'd never known him give up on a manhunt, no matter what it cost.

All that long ride home Nate racked his brain to figure out what he could have done different, how six men could have outwitted three or four. In that damned canyon the outlaws couldn't be reached; if he'd tried to attack them he'd only have led the posse into an ambush.

Always he came back to the same answer; Nate didn't know how, but Jeff would have found a way. He wasn't even sure if he'd been right to leave Eli behind with Louis and Jim, to keep Cord and his gang closed up in the canyon while he was gone.

Guilt rode pillion, whispering at Nate's shoulder. He'd been flattered when the town council offered him the badge, but he never should have taken the job. As the one-time sheriff's friend he should have locked Jeff up until he quit the drink, not turned him loose time after time, knowing he'd be back in jail after the next drunken brawl.

'Sheriff?' Bronc broke in on his gloom. The cowboy was pale and gaunt from the pain of his wound, but his arm looked like it was healing clean. He'd kept pace with the sheriff, refusing to take the ride at an easier pace. 'What happened to Monty,' he said quietly, 'that weren't your fault. He knowed better than to stand up an' show hisself that way. Call it bad luck.'

'Wish I could,' Nate replied. 'Way I see it, I haven't done a damn thing right. Didn't even take enough supplies. If Eli hadn't tracked down that buck he and the others would have their bellies scraping their backbones by now. As for Monty, I shouldn't have sent either of you up there to get shot at.' He sighed. 'Once we hit town I'll be looking to make up another posse. Take ropes with us maybe.'

'You don't figure to climb down into Hell's Gate?' Bronc asked.

'Darned if I know. One thing's for sure. If we can only flush 'em out of the canyons I'll track 'em to hell and gone if I have to.'

Nate lapsed back into silence. Trouble

was, he couldn't think of more than three other men who'd join him. When Jeff Warrinder had called for volunteers there'd always been a couple of dozen queuing up to be deputized. There'd be a lot of hard talk when folks heard he'd ridden back a man short and with the fugitives still on the loose. He'd have to telegraph to Burville and ask for help. They owed him, he thought bitterly; if they'd sent the marshals to fetch Ross Cord the way they should then none of this would have happened.

In the distance Redemption came in sight, high on the bluff. Nate kicked his weary mount to a lope, a sour taste in his mouth. Defeat was a hard thing to swallow.

'Rider comin',' Bronc said. 'Looks like Bull Krantz on that big grey of his.'

Nate nodded. They'd been on Double Bar K land for the last hour. He grimaced; the size of the Krantz's outfit they could have spared him six men and barely noticed it, but it'd be a rare day when that family went out of their way to back the law.

Bull Krantz turned the tall grey horse round and pulled up in the sheriff's path. 'This is convenient, Sheriff. We need to talk.'

'Sure we do.' Nate curbed his own mount and stared at the big man. It would be good to shift some of the blame for all that had gone wrong over the last few days on to this man's broad shoulders.

'First chance I've had to say this, Mr Krantz. Next time you bring in a rustler you talk to me first, instead of throwing your weight around in my office when I'm not there.'

The old rancher pretended surprise. 'You talking about that Hanson woman?'

Nate Grundy nodded. 'She never should have been locked up in the jail. I got enough on my plate, without wondering if there's a woman lying dead in the river, or out there in the hands of Ross Cord and his gang.'

Bull threw back his huge head and

roared with laughter. 'You thought they took her? You've been wasting your time, sheriff; you were looking in the wrong place. Cassie Hanson's back on that run-down spread of hers. Last I saw, the shameless bitch was getting real cosy with the town drunk.'

'What?'

'Sorry,' the older man didn't sound it. 'I was forgetting that bum's a friend of yours.'

Nate drove his horse closer. 'Are you saying Jeff Warrinder's still alive?'

Bull shrugged. 'Sure. Though she must be keeping him short of liquor; he looks like somebody dug him up a couple of days after they buried him. And he's got the shakes real bad.'

'But what's he doing at the Lazy Zee?'

'Talk is, the woman saved his neck the night they got broke out of jail.' Bull's heavy features attempted a smile. 'Makes your job a whole lot easier, Sheriff, you can go arrest them both at once.'

'There's no charge out against either

one of them,' Nate said, thinking fast. 'If you want to complain about Mrs Hanson then you come and do it all proper and legal. Providing there's a case to answer I'll draw up a warrant, but even so it'll have to wait a week or two, I've still got three outlaws to track down.'

'Isn't that what you went out to do?' Bull reined the stallion back hard and the horse half-reared as he dragged its head towards the Double Bar K. 'Don't you worry yourself over Mrs Hanson, Sheriff, she won't be helping herself to any more of my cattle. Young Rupe's away just now, but soon as he gets back he'll be taking good care of her. And he'll maybe settle Warrinder's hash at the same time.' With that he released his hold on the rein and the stallion bounded into motion.

* * *

The Lazy Zee lay quiet in the afternoon heat, only the rhythmic tap of a hammer breaking the silence. Nate

Grundy kneed his horse around the house, looking for the source of the sound. A man was hammering a sheet of corrugated iron to the wall of a ramshackle lean-to. Hearing the hoof-beats he half-turned.

'Nate!' Jeff Warrinder threw down the hammer, his face lighting up. 'Sure am glad to see you.' He took in the trail dust and the expression on the sheriff's face. 'You didn't get 'em.'

Nate Grundy shook his head. He climbed wearily out of the saddle. 'Tried to drive them out of Hell's Gate canyon by getting up on the ridge, but it didn't work. I lost a man. Young cowpoke by the name of Monty. Used to work for the Double Bar K.'

'That place sure has the right name. I heard there were just six of you rode out. Not enough to root three men out of Hell's Gate, it might have been made for scum like Cord to hole up in. You were lucky not to lose more.'

'I know it.' Nate led his horse to the trough. While it drank he studied his

121

friend, noting the way Jeff Warrinder's fists were clenched. The bruises on his face suggested he'd been fighting again; maybe Bull had it wrong, maybe the man was still drinking. And yet there was something different about him. Warrinder's features showed a tranquillity that had been missing since his wife died.

'I had my reasons for staying, Jeff. I thought you were dead. By the signs, we reckoned Jeremiah Brodie tipped you into the river, and that they took Mrs Hanson along for the ride. Didn't learn different until I met Bull Krantz just now. He told me I'd find the pair of you here.'

'Guess that laid an extra burden on you.' Jeff put a hand on the younger man's shoulder, and Nate felt it shaking before it was quickly withdrawn. 'I'm real sorry.'

'I'll be going back. Left three men keeping watch so Cord can't sneak out of there.'

There was a spell of quietness, the

two men thinking their own thoughts. Jeff shook himself and thrust his thumbs into his belt in an attempt to hide the tremors.

'Mrs Hanson saved my neck, Nate,' he said at last. 'Nearly got herself drowned doing it. After that I couldn't turn my back on her. A place like this is too much for a woman on her own, I've been paying my debt with a few days' hard labour.'

'That's not the way Bull Krantz tells it.'

Warrinder's mouth twisted. 'He measures the whole world by his own crooked standards. Man can't be in two places at once, but I should've been out at Hell's Gate with you, sure wish I had been.'

'You saying you're fit to ride?'

'I haven't touched a drink since that night.' He grimaced. 'Kind of late to try fixing things, no reason why the town should take me back, but I'd be willing to sign on as your deputy. Be grateful if you'd give me the chance, Nate.'

'I could sure use you. It'll take me a

while to put another posse together though.'

Jeff Warrinder nodded. 'You'll have to stake me to a horse and a gun, but I'd be happy to help put a rope round the neck of the bastard who killed old Abe.'

Nate put up a hand and touched the dusty scrap of metal pinned to his vest. 'Won't seem right, me wearing this badge with you along. These last few days taught me some lessons.'

'If you're man enough to admit that then I got no complaints,' Jeff told him. 'I finish up here tomorrow. I'll come into town the day after and you can swear me in.'

9

Rupe Krantz eased down from his horse outside the Jack of Clubs saloon, tipping his hat back as he walked up the steps from the street, pushing through the idlers hanging round the door. Though it was several days since his encounter with Jeff Warrinder, Rupe's nose was still red and swollen, but it would take a brave man to comment on it.

He threw coins at the barman, downing three glasses of whiskey in quick succession. When he was done he strode back out to his horse. Facing his father wasn't something Rupe cared to do stone cold sober, though he had to get the balance right; if he drank too much the old man was likely to take a belt to him, no matter that he'd been full grown these past five years.

Rupe's mood lightened a little as he rode out of Redemption past the cabin that had once belonged to Jeff War-rinder. It stood empty and neglected. There was talk that the man who'd bought it was going to build a cat house, or maybe a gambling joint; with Warrinder no longer wearing a star the town was beginning to holler again. Rupe preferred it that way, and he liked to think that all Warrinder's efforts had been for nothing.

The hands at the Double Bar K were returning from their day's work and the place was bustling with men tending their horses, standing gabbing by the barn or washing up outside the bunkhouse. Rupe dismounted, throwing the chestnut's reins to one of the wranglers. He wasn't pleased to see Bull striding out of the barn, he'd hoped to keep their confrontation private.

'You been avoiding me, boy? Didn't you want to come home?' Bull Krantz stood square, a great crag of a man facing Rupe across the yard. The cowboys who'd been milling around a minute before were suddenly gone, keeping their distance from the boss, leaving father and son alone. They'd be watching and listening from the cover of the barn and the bunkhouse, grateful that Bull's fury wasn't turned on them.

'I don't know what you're talking about.' Rupe was sullen.

'I'm talking about you lying to me! Must be a month ago since I sent you to talk to that Hanson woman. How come she never heard about the offer I told you to make?'

'I talked to her.'

Bull snorted, sounding more beast than man. 'What about? Did you ask for her recipe for apple pie?'

'I did what you said.' Rupe lied. He could almost feel the pairs of eyes boring into his back. He hunched his shoulders, hating the hidden watchers for seeing his humiliation.

'I can't believe I spawned a son with so little backbone,' Bull said contemptuously. 'And what about this time? One day you'll own the Double Bar K, but I'm not sure you're man enough, the way you let that drunken bum throw you out.'

The whiskey had lit a fire in Rupe's belly. He looked at his father, hating the assurance in his eyes, the unshakeable belief that he was stronger than any other man in creation. The old man took a step closer. That was when Rupe saw the bruises. Somebody had marked Bull Krantz! It was as if the river had suddenly started to run backwards; the whole of his landscape changed in that second. No man had ever given his father a beating!

'Reckon we should talk about this inside,' Rupe said mildly, staring at the damage somebody had done to his father's face. 'You can't be feeling so good. Bet that smarts.'

With a roar Bull came for him, hands reaching for Rupe's wrist. It was an old trick, but it never failed. He would take hold and toss his opponent around and over one knee in a move that was impossible to escape. Only this time

Rupe didn't stand and wait. He dropped his head and charged, fists flying.

Bull stopped dead in his tracks, seeming to root his feet to the ground. The hands that had been extended to grip were suddenly transformed into knuckled fists like lumps of granite. He shrugged off the haymaker that took him on the chin and ploughed a fist into his son's throat. Rupe's body arced in agony and he dropped at his father's feet, choking painfully, his face flushing dark red, his fingers fluttering helplessly at his neck.

'We'll talk later when you've calmed down,' Bull said. 'Jeff Warrinder said you needed to learn some manners; I hate to admit it but he was right.' He turned away.

Groaning, Rupe climbed to his knees, staring at the retreating back, his eyes filled with an impotent hatred. This was all the fault of the Hanson bitch. Her and Jeff Warrinder. He'd see they got what was coming to them.

* ★ ★

'I don't like to leave you here on your own.' Jeff Warrinder leaned down from the saddle, steadying the black mare as she moved beneath him. The sun was high; he'd meant to leave sooner but even now he was reluctant. He didn't want to let go of Cassie's hand. 'Sure you'll be all right if Bull or Rupe come calling?'

She laughed. 'I've dealt with a few rats in my time, don't worry. Besides, the sheriff promised to warn them off.'

'Yeah, but that won't hold once he's on the way to Hell's Gate with the posse.' He hesitated, his face unreadable as he met her look. 'After Sarah I never thought I'd feel this way again.'

'Oh, Jeff. Me and Steve . . . ' Cassie's cheeks were pink. 'I guess what's between us is meant to be. I don't think either Steve or Sarah would mind. They'd want us to be happy.'

'Maybe. But Sarah's death was my fault. I don't figure I could face it if anything happened to you.'

'We can't spend our whole lives being afraid,' she said gently. She put a foot on the toe of his boot and leapt up to kiss him swiftly on the mouth. Once her feet were back on the ground she laughed.

'There's always Steve's shotgun. I'll keep both barrels loaded. That reminds me . . . ' She ran into the ranch house, coming back a minute later carrying a revolver wrapped in a gunbelt. Jeff took the weapon, removing it from the holster; he didn't recognize the model. He spun the chambers; although the gun was old it had been well cared for.

'It's a .32,' Cassie said. 'It belonged to my father, and it was old when he bought it, but he swore it shot true.' She handed him a box of ammunition. 'Here. I wish I had a rifle to give you. Won't you keep the mare?'

He leant down and kissed the top of her head. 'You might need her. Tell Tree to pick her up from the livery in the morning. Don't worry, Nate'll see me right.' He pushed the black into motion, then reined in when he reached the gate, turning to look back.

'What we talked about last night . . . I don't want to rush you none, you're sure it's what you want?'

She flushed again, smiling. 'You know it. We'll see the preacher as soon as you get back.'

★   ★   ★

Jeff Warrinder pushed open the door of the office that had once been his.

'Howdy, Jeff, glad you could make it,' Nate Grundy said, grinning widely. 'With the three men I left out at Hell's Gate that makes ten of us. Should be just about enough.'

Five men were grouped round the desk where Nate sat. Two of them Jeff didn't recognize. One of the strangers was a tall, thin man, dressed in a deerskin coat with fringes hanging from the shoulders. As Jeff came in he turned, his expression less than welcoming.

132

Nate stood. 'This here's Marshal Darbo from Burville. He'll be riding with us in the morning.' He turned to the stranger. 'Marshal, I guess you haven't met Jeff Warrinder.'

'Warrinder?' Darbo's sharp features contracted. 'I heard — ' He broke off. 'You were sheriff here in Redemption.'

'I was.' Jeff kept his voice even. 'But right now I've come to be sworn in as a deputy. Any objections?'

Darbo shrugged. 'This is Sheriff Grundy's operation. Me and Deputy Kemp are just along to lend a hand.'

Kemp nodded a greeting. He was a fat man, and the top of his head barely reached Darbo's shoulder. A smile lit his fleshy face. 'Can't have too many men on a job like this,' he said.

Jeff found himself returning the smile. 'I'd say you got that right.' He looked round at the familiar faces. There was Jim Ormond's cousin Herb, along with Shorty Sims, six foot eight if he was an inch, but not over bright, and Joe Detelli, who was more at home with a deck of cards in his hands than a rifle.

Detelli winked as he caught Jeff's look. 'Been on a losing streak,' he admitted. 'But don't worry, Jeff, I've been practising. Hit the target five times out of six these days.'

'Yeah, so long as you ain't no more than three feet away,' Shorty guffawed.

'At least I can tell a grizzly bear from a barn door,' Detelli shot back, bringing up an incident in Sims's past he'd rather forget.

'That's enough,' Sheriff Grundy said. 'You want to fight, save it for the men waiting for us at Hell's Gate. Those of you who aren't already sworn in, raise your right hands.'

Once the brief formality was over Grundy handed the newcomers the scraps of tin that identified them as deputies. 'We meet on the street outside here at first light. And don't be late.'

Once the others had gone Jeff sat in the visitor's chair in Grundy's office, cradling a cup of coffee and looking across at his friend.

'What are you thinking?' Nate asked.

Jeff shrugged, gripping the cup hard as a tremor ran through his fingers. 'That with two other professional lawmen and old Eli along we've got a chance,' he said. 'So long as there's only Cord, Brodie and one more up there, like you reckon, we might be able to take 'em.' He swallowed a mouthful of coffee. 'Half-a-dozen well-armed men could hold us off for months. You know anything about Darbo and Kemp?'

'I'm told they're good at their job.' Nate got up and poured himself more coffee, sitting himself back down and putting his feet on the desk. 'Darbo says he's just tagging along, but maybe he won't be too happy taking orders.'

'I'll back you, Nate, don't worry. I'd keep the others paired off as much as possible, save them thinking about getting scared.'

Nate nodded. 'Makes sense. You reckon it'll work, going in from the top of the ridge? They know we managed to get up there; could be they'll be

135

watching for us. One of 'em's damn good with a rifle, the way he took out Monty and Bronc.'

'It's risky. Dark might help. We could let ourselves down from the top at night, hole up until dawn, but they know the territory, we could just be setting ourselves up to give 'em some target practice.'

Jeff tipped his hat back and rubbed a hand across his forehead. 'There's something been nagging at the back of my mind, maybe it'll come clear in the morning. Got a bit of an idea anyway. Reckon I might need to call in a favour from Al Green; no point telling you more unless it pans out.'

'Sure.' Nate hesitated, staring at his boots propped up on the desk. 'You staying in town tonight?'

Jeff grinned. 'Dave Lensky says I can bed down at the livery. Got kind of used to keeping Cassie Hanson's little mare company. Don't fret none, I don't even have the price of a beer on me.'

'Never gave it a thought,' Nate lied

cheerfully. 'Once I've finished the rounds tonight I figure to eat at the hotel; since you're flat broke you'd better join me.'

He lifted a hand to silence Jeff's protest. 'You can owe me till you've earned your pay.'

★   ★   ★

Redemption lay under a quarter moon, only a faint murmur of sound reaching the deserted street from inside the Jack of Clubs. As Jeff stalked past a couple of men appeared at the door. One of them was Rupe Krantz.

'Hey, Warrinder. Why don't I buy you a drink?' Rupe's shout followed him, but Jeff didn't look round, steering straight for the livery stables. He was never going down that road again.

The livery barn stood open, lit only by a lantern hanging outside. Jeff pushed the door most of the way shut and felt his way to the black mare's stall. The horse snorted a greeting. Jeff propped the rifle Nate Grundy had given him against the wall, and laid out the bedroll he'd brought with him from the Lazy Zee. He unbuckled his gunbelt and put it on the straw close to hand.

Sleep refused to come. Jeff stared at the patch of light beyond the door where the lantern flickered; the craving was still with him, gnawing at his gut. It had been easier out at the ranch, when the nearest drink was over an hour's ride away. Thoughts of the Lazy Zee brought Cassie to mind, and he armed himself with the memory of her, smiling when he recalled the way she'd climbed up to kiss him before he left. He clenched his fists. A girl like that was worth a few sleepless nights.

The mare whinnied and stamped uneasily. On the verge of sleep Jeff cursed. 'Of all the damn fool, lop-eared, four-legged critters . . . ' His eyes ached. He bunched the blanket round him, wishing he could lay himself out cold for a few hours.

Jeff sat up as the mare struck again at

the floor with a restless hoof. He was suddenly wide awake. The scent of smoke was drifting through the barn and there was sound that could have been the crackle of fire. Outside, the lantern swayed a little as a gentle breeze blew. The moon sent a cold sheen over the empty street, but there was a warmer glow too, flickering against the wall of the drug-store opposite. Jeff turned to look for its source.

'Jeez!' A crimson light was flickering through gaps in the planking at the back of the barn. Jeff ran out into the street and around the side of the building. As he skirted the barn the breath went out of him in sudden relief. The fire was well clear of the livery, a great bright beacon built on an empty patch of ground at the very edge of the bluff. Nobody seemed to be tending the flames, but the blaze posed no threat to the town.

Jeff turned to go back to his bedroll. In the split second when common sense, dulled by the months of boozing, told him he'd been a fool, something struck him hard between the shoulder blades. He went down fast, with no time to save himself from hitting the ground head first. Pain shot from his head to the end of his backbone, taking in a whole lot of territory in between. Bright lights flashed across his vision, and when the fireworks were over the world went dark.

10

'Careful!' The word was hissed in venomous fury. 'I want him alive an' awake.'

Jeff's fuddled brain told him to move, but the message never had time to reach his legs. Several pairs of hands took hold of him and pulled him upright. He tried to swing a punch at one of the vague shapes milling around but the effect was laughable; he would have fallen but for the men holding him.

'The barn's real handy,' a man said quietly.

'No, we're playing safe,' came the whispered reply. 'We'll take him down where I said. Put something in his mouth to keep him quiet.'

'Sure thing, boss.'

Jeff's bandanna was untied from his neck and thrust between his teeth. It tasted of trail dirt and stale whiskey. A grain sack was pulled down over his head and pulled tight around his neck and the darkness became total again. Although the words had been spoken in a whisper the voice giving the orders was familiar. With a shiver of something akin to fear, Jeff recognized it. Rupe Krantz!

He didn't resist as they carried him down the hill. The pain in his skull was fading to a dull ache, and the dizziness was passing. Jeff acted more helpless than he felt, letting them take his weight with his boots dragging; his attackers hadn't tied his arms and legs, which meant he might have a chance to fight or run once they loosed their hold. From the grip of their hands and the sound of scuffling feet he tried to work out how many men there were, and came up with five or six. That wasn't good.

How long they were moving Jeff couldn't tell. The feel of the air changed. There was a sharper breeze, cold on his hands. He realized they were close to the river; he could hear the rustle of water over stones.

'This'll do.' Rupe wasn't bothering to keep his voice down now they were clear of the town. 'Keep a good hold when I take this off, we don't want him going for a swim; that's how he got away from Cord.'

The sack was pulled off Jeff's head. A bright shaft of moonlight lay across the dark surface of the river, almost at his feet. They were under the bluff below the town, a little way upstream from the crossing. Jeff bunched his muscles, ready to throw off the men who held him and make a run for it, but Rupe gave him no chance. He stepped forward, a pistol in his hand. With exaggerated care he cocked the gun and set the barrel against Jeff's neck, while with his other hand he removed the bandanna from Jeff's mouth.

'Just so's you don't dccide to leave the party early,' Rupe said, an unpleasant grin on his face. 'Not that I'll kill you, a slug in the foot will do. You want to try it?' He laughed. 'No? Fine. Pull him down, boys.'

Jeff was helpless. They dragged him backwards until his spine fetched up against a rock, then they kept pulling until he lay angled across it, his arms stretched uncomfortably back around the stone in a painful embrace.

'I'm real sociable,' Rupe said, stepping closer. 'I get hurt when a man won't take a drink with me. What's the matter, *Mister* Warrinder, you think you're too good to share my whiskey?' He held up a bottle, the smile on his face widening. 'A week ago you weren't so damn proud.'

Jeff's legs were still free. At the cost of a few torn muscles in arms and shoulders already strained to the point of agony, he heaved his lower torso off the rock and let fly with his feet. One boot caught Rupe Krantz in the stomach with a satisfyingly soggy thud, while the other hit the shin of one of the men who held his arms. Grunting with the effort Jeff ripped himself free in the split second when the man's grip loosened, rolling sideways over the rock to slam a fist at the cowboy on his other side.

As if from nowhere a hand grabbed Jeff by the throat, huge fingers taking a tight grip. The haymaker he'd aimed at the man to his right evaporated like mist on a summer day. To move would be to increase the agonizing pressure on his neck; to move would be to die. More hands grasped his arms and within seconds he was spread-eagled again, out of options.

In time Rupe came back into his sight. He wasn't smiling any more, but he still held the bottle. 'No more games, Warrinder. Somebody get those boots off him.'

When Jeff's feet were bare Rupe took a step back, then stamped hard. Jeff bit down on the agony that exploded across his toes and up his leg.

'Now,' Rupe said. 'Reckon we need that rope.'

Jeff made it hard for them, but it only earned him a few more bruises. They tied him at wrists and ankles, stretching his arms and legs around the rock again until he thought his joints would be wrenched apart. The man who'd held him by the throat took a fresh grip, this time pinching Jeff's nose.

Rupe loomed over him. 'You're going to take a drink with me, Warrinder.' The mouth of the bottle jarred against Jeff's teeth and tilted. Still he fought, refusing to swallow. The fiery liquor flowed into his windpipe and he choked. He couldn't stop a little of the whiskey trickling down his throat. It tasted good. He cursed inwardly. It was like coming to a waterhole after a week in the desert; he needed liquor like he needed air to breathe. Jeff thought of Cassie and did his best to spit it back out.

'I brought plenty,' Rupe said, the smile back on his face as his victim spluttered. 'You've got two choices, Warrinder: you swallow it, or you drown in it.'

Joe Detelli heaved on the cinch and the horse shifted its weight as the bellyband tightened. Joe swore comprehensively in Italian as a shod hoof landed on the toe of his boot.

He led the bay out on to the dark street, pausing by the livery barn and staring in through the wide-open door. 'Jeff?' He peered into the shadows cast by the lantern. 'Time we were going, Jeff.'

There was no response. Hitching his horse to the rail Detelli lifted the lamp down and took it inside. The straw rustled as the black mare turned to look at him. A humped shape lay at her feet, half covered by a blanket. Joe Detelli bent down, straightening again sharply as the powerful smell of whiskey reached him, along with a quiet rhythmic snore.

Detelli shook his head and returned to the street. A horse stood saddled outside the sheriff's office; Nate's black. There was a faint glow in the eastern sky; the rest of the posse would be assembling soon. As Detelli approached, Nate Grundy came down the steps and slid the Enfield into its holster.

The sheriff nodded a greeting. 'G' morning Joe.'

'Not so good,' Detelli said. 'Come see what I found.'

Nate turned Jeff Warrinder over. The man muttered incoherently, his eyes tight shut, one hand flopping away from his body, releasing an empty bottle that clinked against the wooden wall. The sheriff cursed. 'How'd he get hold of that? He swore he didn't have the price of a beer.'

'Shall we try to sober him up?'

'In half an hour? No chance. How's it gonna look if we set off with him tied to his saddle? Besides, he's no use to me with a skinful.' Nate looked around. 'I gave Jeff the Winchester out of the office last night, but I don't see it. I guess that's where he got the booze.'

'You think he sold your rifle?' Detelli said doubtfully.

'I told you, he was broke. I should have known better.' He aimed a none-too-gentle kick at Warrinder's backside. The man merely grunted and turned away from him. 'Folk used to say Jeff Warrinder was worth two men. We'll be kinda short of manpower.'

'We could wait?' Detelli suggested. 'For more help?'

'No, I didn't like leaving Eli and the others; we need to get back out there.'

'What shall we do about Jeff?' Joe Detelli asked, as he followed Grundy back across the street.

'Nothing,' Nate said bleakly. 'Far as I'm concerned he's through.'

The rest of the posse were gathered in the street, hats pulled down and collars high against the morning chill. Grundy greeted the other men, counting heads; even with three deputies waiting at Hell's Gate it didn't look near enough for what he had in mind. He pushed the thought away. 'Mount up, boys, let's go hunting.'

149

Redemption woke up and went about its business. The sun travelled across the cloudless sky and just before midday a bright shaft of light found its way through a chink above the door of the livery barn, where a plank had warped. Jeff Warrinder groaned and screwed his eyes shut a little harder as the brightness battered at his lids. It was a disappointment to find he was still alive; death would have been preferable to opening his eyes on yet another morning.

As always Jeff's first thought was of Sarah, his second that she was dead, and that he'd killed her. Then the pain hit him; he hurt all over. Hell, even his teeth hurt. Something vile rose in his gorge, threatening to choke him. Sheer physical discomfort drove thoughts of his wife from his mind.

Somebody kicked him in the small of his back. 'Big man!' The voice familiar but he couldn't place it.

Thinking was hard with a swarm of bees buzzing around his brain, every one of them stinging him from the inside.

'I warn her, but Mrs Hanson trust you.'

Cassie? His brain formed the word but he couldn't get it through to his mouth. He hitched himself on to his elbows and threw up, his body heaving. The bees turned into an army of ants, all of them wearing boots and marching in step. Memory seeped back. Reluctantly he tilted his head and opened one eye. A familiar pair of worn moccasins filled his vision. Tree. The half-breed spat expressively, then turned to go.

Jeff was beginning to recall a few things about the night before. Foremost among them was Rupe Krantz. There'd been something he said. Something about the Lazy Zee . . . In desperation he lunged, catching hold of Tree's ankle. He brought the old man to a stumbling halt so suddenly that Tree almost fell.

A gnarled hand chopped at his arm

and Jeff gasped. The pain was out of all proportion to the strength of the blow, but he didn't let go, his mind running doggedly on a single thought. 'Rupe . . .' The word came out as a desperate whisper. 'Tree, tell Mrs Hanson . . . '

'Tell her what?' Tree hunkered down beside Jeff. There was a silence, then his long fingers tugged the sleeve up from Jeff's wrist. 'He do this? Young Krantz?'

Jeff tried to nod but it hurt too much. The old half-breed pulled away the blanket that was tangled round Jeff's feet. There was a long silence. Jeff thought the old man had gone, but then a hand half lifted him, and a trickle of water ran into his mouth. 'Too many times I do this,' Tree said. 'What I say to Mrs Hanson?'

'Rupe. He's awful mad. Got a thrashing from his pa . . . Bull wants the Lazy Zee . . . '

Tree nodded slowly. 'I say this already, but she not listen good.' He stared at the rope burns on Jeff's ankles, and the bruises on his feet.

'Krantz makes bad enemy. I tell her what he do here.'

'No. Don't tell her that; I'm fine.' Jeff closed his eyes. When his head cleared, then perhaps he'd find Rupe Krantz and beat the hell out of him, but that would have to wait a while. Nausea struck him again; for now he just wanted to be left alone to die in peace. 'Go away,' he muttered.

He heard nothing more, drifting into the familiar half-world between drunk and sober, wishing he could pass out for a few more hours. An image came into his mind. A tall man, a friend, smiling and handing him a rifle as he said something about the morning. That was when he recalled the promise he'd made to Nate Grundy.

'Jeez!' He was supposed to be on his way to Hell's Gate. Nate didn't know about the idea he'd had, or about the favour Jeff had called in from old man Greenwood. He'd got to go. He had an appointment with a posse.

By concentrating hard, Jeff managed

to climb to hands and knees, and he waited there awhile until the barn floor steadied beneath him. His mouth was dust dry; he recalled there was a trough out the back. It took several minutes to get to his feet; he was surprised to find that he'd lost his boots. His right foot hurt like crazy when he put weight on it, but he limped outside and plunged his head and shoulders into the water, gripping the edge of the trough hard so he didn't fall in.

When he came back up he found himself looking at a short, spare, old man in a striped shirt and denim dungarees.

'Looks like I got off light,' Dave Lensky said. 'You all right, boy?'

'What?' Jeff stared blearily at him, then at Tree who was standing in the doorway of Lensky's cabin across the yard.

'They left me tied up,' Dave said. 'Guess they didn't want to be disturbed.' His nose wrinkled. 'Sure spread that whiskey wide, you smell

154

worse'n Pusey's shit house.'

Jeff grunted. 'You must've seen the fire . . . '

'I saw it right enough. I lay there thinkin' they was ready to roast me in my own bed! I didn't get a look at 'em but I heard enough to know who they was. It was Rupe Krantz and some of the boys from the Double Bar K.'

Jeff began to nod, stopping abruptly as the booted ants resumed their march. 'I owe Rupe an evening's hospitality.'

Dave Lensky snorted, rubbing his stiffened arms. 'Ain't no way to treat a man at my time of life neither. Bull shoulda come down hard on that boy a long time ago. But I guess it's the same bad blood runs through the pair of 'em. Sure wish you was still sheriff, Jeff. When you catch up with that kid you give him a couple from me.'

'My pleasure.'

'You don't look good,' the old man said. 'Anythin' I can do to help?'

'Sure. Work the pump. I gotta chase

this liquor out of my head. Then I'll need some strong coffee and a horse.'

'What about Krantz?'

'Rupe'll have to wait, I'm supposed to be out with the posse.'

11

'Bad idea,' Tree said laconically, as he helped Jeff Warrinder into the saddle. Jeff clung to the horn and waited for the world to stop spinning; he wanted to puke again though his stomach was empty.

'No business of yours. You sure that rifle's gone?' Maybe Nate had come looking for him and reclaimed the Winchester; if not then Rupe had it, which made just one more thing to settle between them when the time came. 'Get back to the Lazy Zee. Tell Mrs Hanson she mustn't stay out there. She'd best move into town — '

'I hear,' Tree interrupted. He led Dave Lensky's horse out of the barn. 'You're one crazy man.'

Jeff pulled the brim of his hat down low as the daylight bored into his eyes, sharp as a knife. He took a couple of deep breaths and the pain receded a little. 'I can do this. Give me the reins.'

Tree seemed not to hear, staring down the street.

'It's a bad time to start playing the dumb redskin; I got a short fuse right now.' Jeff said. When Tree didn't answer he followed the half-breed's gaze and saw the big man riding towards them, instantly recognizable on the tall grey stallion. Tree turned the borrowed horse around as if to lead him back to the livery.

'No,' Jeff said, straightening in the saddle. 'I've got things to say to Bull Krantz.'

In silence, Tree tossed him the rein and Jeff kneed the animal into the rancher's path. Bull looked Jeff over and nodded, a half smile on his craggy features. 'I heard you fell off the wagon.'

'Didn't fall exactly,' Jeff replied. 'I'd say I was pushed.'

'Helped, maybe. Don't kid yourself. When a man's got a weakness it'll always show. Rupe only speeded things up some.'

'We'll argue this out another time,' Jeff said. 'Be obliged if you'd give that boy of yours a message. Tell him I'll be sure to repay his hospitality, just as soon as I get back.'

'Is that a threat, Warrinder?' Bull's face darkened.

'I don't trade in threats,' Jeff replied. 'You can tell Rupe it's a promise. He was kind enough to treat me to a couple of bottles of whiskey, so next time it'll be my turn. Reckon I'd like to see him eat crow. And tell him I'll be sure the odds aren't six to one in his favour. He's built wrong for a coward, sure must be a disappointment to you.'

Bull's right hand dropped from the rein and bunched over the butt of his six-gun. He pushed the stallion closer, but stopped as Dave Lensky came out of his barn, an ancient rifle in his hands.

'Your son stepped over the line last night, Bull,' the old liveryman said.

'Whole town knows about it. You leave Jeff be.'

The rancher scowled and looked around. Al Green stood outside the store, his thumbs hooked into the belt of his apron, a couple of customers behind him, while downhill a small crowd had gathered on the sidewalk by the hotel. All of their eyes were on him.

'Later, Warrinder,' Krantz growled. He wrenched the stallion's head around and jogged on up the street towards the bank.

Jeff touched his hat to Dave and rode off in the opposite direction, kicking the horse to a lope and gritting his teeth against the pain the movement awoke in half-a-dozen parts of his body. A ragged cheer followed him as he turned the corner down towards the river. The sound lifted his spirits; one day maybe he'd hold his head high again in the streets of Redemption. For a brief moment he felt almost human.

The good feeling didn't last. It was tempting to let the horse drop back to a walk when the wave of nausea hit him, but Jeff gritted his teeth and plugged on, though his mount's ground-eating lope jarred through him. Hell's Gate Canyon lay more than a day's ride ahead, and he'd have to push hard to reach it before Nate got himself into trouble. The more he thought about it the crazier it seemed to try storming the outlaw's hideout, either from the top of the ridge, or from the mouth of Hell's Gate. The memory he'd been questing for the previous day was coming clear, emerging from the fog that the months of boozing had left in his brain. Jeff kicked the horse to a faster pace; he didn't want to be too late to prevent a massacre.

By the time darkness fell, Jeff was barely conscious. He slid off the horse by the side of a water-hole and watched the animal drink, then he hitched it to a rock, doling out a few handfuls of grain for the weary beast. Instead of lowering its head to eat the horse neighed, ears pricked as it stared back down the trail.

It took Jeff almost a minute to make out what the animal had heard; there was another horse coming, slow and hesitant in the uncertain light. Jeff drew the ancient gun Cassie had given him and took a few silent steps away from his mount, listening to the soft hesitant thud of approaching hoofs.

'Ride on in,' he called harshly, 'good and slow.'

'Jeff?' Cassie Hanson called uncertainly. 'Is that you?'

'What in the name of tarnation are you doing out here?' Jeff winced at the sound of his own voice. He rubbed his eyes, staring at the apparition just visible by the dim starlight. 'You're plain crazy riding so far alone!'

Cassie Hanson stepped down off the black mare, her back ramrod straight as she faced him, her face a pale oval in the darkness within its halo of fair hair. 'I came because I had to.' She stepped closer. The little mare moved past her to snuffle in friendship at the man

162

who'd shared her stall for the past week.

'Jeff, you're hurt . . . '

He snorted. 'You think I'm some dumb kid? Listen, lady, when I feel the need of a nursemaid — '

Cassie slapped his face so suddenly Jeff had no time to dodge, and the power of the blow made him stagger. He grabbed hold of the black's saddle horn to steady himself. Coming on top of all the damage Rupe's boys had inflicted the attack was enough to set his head ringing.

'Yes, you're dumb! I didn't ride all this way to soothe your sore head, though a fine lot of thanks you'd give me if I had! Rupe's on my tail.'

'He's what?' Jeff stared past her, back into the darkness. Above all else he'd been concerned to keep Cassie Hanson safe, during the torment of the day's riding it had been his one comfort, that she was back in Redemption, and among friends.

Her expression softened. 'I couldn't

163

help it Jeff, I'm sorry. When Tree told me what had happened I headed for town. I was going to visit with Mrs Borovsky for a few days while you were gone, like you said, only Rupe and his boys were waiting. I was lucky, the mare scented their horses and I circled round them. They didn't see me take the trail down by the river. If they had they'd have caught me.'

'Then this is the last place you ought to be! You'd have been safe in town — '

'Without you or Nate Grundy there? I doubt it. Listen, we're wasting time. They're only a mile or so back. We'd better move on.'

It was hard to concentrate. Jeff drew a hand across his forehead, trying to wipe away the whiskey haze in his mind. He spun the cylinder of the old revolver, holding it close to his eyes so he could check that the chambers were loaded.

'There's an arroyo running to the east of us,' he said, 'about half a mile off the trail. It's deep enough to hide you and the mare, but don't let her make a noise. And keep your head down.' He looked around for the nearest patch of cover; there was nothing but a few stunted junipers. 'Shame there's no time to light a fire. If Rupe's come all this way I ought to get the coffee boiling and give him a proper welcome.'

'Now who's crazy? There's three of them. And you can hardly stand up straight with all that liquor still washing around your insides. Besides, I'm not leaving you. We go together, or we stay together.' She touched his arm, suddenly urgent. 'There'll be time enough to deal with Rupe, but not now, Jeff, and not alone. Please.'

He put his hand over hers. 'I'm not thinking straight. Don't worry, there'll be no shooting.' A shiver ran through him. The last time he'd fired a gun had been the day his life fell apart.

The events of the previous night were none too clear in Jeff's head, but he remembered well enough what Rupe's plans for Cassie Hanson were. He fought down the anger that the memory aroused. He'd deal with Rupe, once Cassie was safely out of the man's reach. 'You think I'd risk anything happening to you?'

Cassie's lips curved into a smile as she turned to the little black horse and reached over its saddle. 'I brought you something, though maybe I ought to wait and give it to you in the morning when you're closer to sober.'

The shotgun caught the faint glimmer of starlight.

'That's a mighty useful gift,' Jeff said as he took the gun. He pulled Cassie to him and kissed her on the lips. A hand came up and caressed the cheek that was still smarting from the slap she'd given him. When they separated Jeff let out a long breath.

'Come on, we'd best get off the trail. We'll find a place to wait out the night, and in the morning as soon as it's safe you're heading back to town.'

She nodded meekly. 'Yes, Jeff.' Despite the danger they were in he could hear the laughter bubbling behind her words. Fear snagged at him. He'd been right, she was crazy. Just the way Sarah had been crazy when she'd refused to get out of the wagon that day.

★ ★ ★

The posse broke camp at first light and headed for the high country, the outline of the hills looming ever closer as they rode. By noon they were riding into the canyons, the high walls white up above where the sun caught them, the shadows at their feet deep and cold. Nate still didn't know what he would do when he reached Hell's Gate.

They'd brought ropes, enough for them to descend to the outlaws' hideout two at a time, but the closer he got the less he liked the idea. They'd have no cover, and going in at night wouldn't make them much safer. Somebody would be standing guard. The marksman in the canyon would only need the light from the camp-fire to show him his target. They'd be dead men before their feet hit the ground.

Nate didn't want to lose more lives. One other plan had half formed in his head. It had the advantage of only putting himself and maybe one other man at risk. Something Eli said had made him think of it; evidently the army's bombardment had killed a couple of the horses belonging to the Meacher gang before they were persuaded to surrender. Maybe the gang realized they wouldn't get far in that kind of territory on foot, even if the army eventually gave up the siege.

Anger at Jeff Warrinder's betrayal fought with the fear lurking at the back of Nate's mind; Jeff had hinted at a plan of his own. Nate wished he could figure it out. Jeff had said something about needing a favour from Al Green, but he already knew they'd be taking ropes. What else could he get from the store that might be useful to them?

Hiding his doubts from the posse,

Nate led the way through the narrowing canyon, coming at last to the campsite by the waterfall, where Eli and Jim waited.

'Sure good to see you,' Eli said. 'Hope you brought some more coffee.'

'Coffee, bacon, beans, grain for the horses,' Nate replied, tossing the old man the pack horse's rein. 'Anything been happening here?'

'Nope. Not heard a peep from 'em. We kept a big fire goin' this side of the arch every night, just like you said, an' there's been one of us watchin', night an' day. They're still in there, Sheriff.' Eli passed the pack horse on to Jim Ormond, who began to unload it.

'Have you been up to the ridge to take another look at them?'

Eli stared up at the tall thin man who had spoken, his forehead furrowing.

'This here's Marshal Darbo from Burville,' Nate said hurriedly. 'He and Deputy Kemp have come along to give us a hand.'

The old man nodded slowly. 'Better

late than never, I guess,' he said. 'And since you ask, no, we didn't climb up to the ridge, seein' as the sheriff told us not to.'

'There's no way they could have got out,' Jim Ormond put in, tearing open a pack of coffee. He winked up at his cousin Herb. 'They're ready an' waitin' for you, Marshal. You go right ahead an' fetch 'em out any time you want.'

Eli grinned and Nate Grundy frowned at him. 'Nobody's going anywhere yet awhile,' he said, stepping down from his horse. 'What I have in mind has to wait for nightfall. Could be worth some of us climbing up to take a looksee first, but not till we've eaten.'

12

'Well?' Nate stared into Darbo's face, trying to make up his mind about the marshal. He'd given a lot of thought to choosing the best men for the plan he had in mind; at least Darbo and Kemp were lawmen. He'd have liked to have Eli backing him up, since he was good with a rifle, but this job would be too much for the old man.

'Can't say I like it,' Darbo said at last, 'but it's your show. Me and Kemp will do it. We'll need somebody who knows the way.'

Nate nodded. 'That'll have to be Louis Jardine.' He stared at the narrow strip of blue sky high above. 'Reckon if you set out in half an hour you'll have plenty of time to pick your spot before dark. Take food and water. You'll need bedrolls; it'll be cold, and you can't light a fire. We can't have 'em knowing you're up there.'

'Sure.'

'We takin' ropes with us?' Louis asked.

'I don't want anyone trying to climb down into the canyon,' Nate said.

'Then why not use the ropes up the gully by the stream?' Louis suggested. 'Make it a whole lot easier when we're on the way back down.'

'Good idea.' Nate looked across the fire at Joe Detelli. 'You OK with this, Joe? If not then I'll try it on my own . . . '

'Hey, I'm a gambling man.' Detelli grinned. 'You know how many towns I've left in the middle of the night? Just hope you can creep in the dark as good as me, Sheriff.'

The rest of the posse stood watching as the three men started up the sloping shelf to the top of the waterfall, their supplies and bedrolls tied on their backs. Eli Ranovich fidgeted at Nate's side, muttering to himself.

'What's the trouble?' Nate asked.

'You been sitting on an ant's nest?'

'Seems to me this plan of yours is full of holes. An' I don't trust Darbo,' Eli growled. 'Don't reckon he likes takin' orders.'

'I'm not asking him to do anything difficult, except maybe climb up there,' he added, nodding at the three figures who were about to go out of sight, pulling themselves up over the lip of stone, alongside the top of the cascade. 'Anyway he's all we've got. Unless we have the boys haul you up that cliff on the end of a rope?'

Nate grinned at the old man's expression. 'Don't worry, reckon you're more use to me here. Me and Joe might need some cover from Hell's Gate if the lead starts flying.'

'An' that's another thing,' Eli grumbled. 'From where we'll be, me an' the other boys are gonna be about as much good to you as a three-legged mule.'

★   ★   ★

173

'They've taken the bait,' Jeff Warrinder lifted his weight off his horse's head and stood up, planting his feet square so he didn't sway when the dizziness hit. The animal snorted its disapproval and heaved upright, shaking itself and showering them with another coating of dust. Beside Jeff, her bright hair dulled and tangled, Cassie loosed her hold on the black mare's rein so it too could climb to its feet, then she rose, slapping dirt from her clothes.

In the far distance a drifting cloud over the Burville trail was all they could see of Rupe and the two men who rode with him. 'You still want me to go back to Redemption?' Cassie asked.

Jeff shook his head. A dull ache reawakened, reminding him of his encounter with Rupe. He was keeping a firm hold on his need for more liquor; his hands weren't shaking yet, but things would get worse before they got better. He needed to get Cassie into safer hands than his, and that meant catching up with Nate and the posse.

'No. You'd best stay where I can keep an eye on you. Once they realize they're following a couple of cowboys heading for a spree in Burville they'll be back, and Rupe'll be mad enough to bust a gut.'

Cassie laughed. 'I wish I could be there when he finds out how we fooled him. So what now?'

He looked up at the sky. They'd spent a long time shaking Rupe off their tracks, and the light would fail them in a couple of hours. 'We won't make Hell's Gate tonight. Best get started though. The sooner we're there the better, you'll be safe from Rupe with the town sheriff and half-a-dozen deputies along.'

'You don't think they'll have trouble catching Cord and the others?' Cassie asked.

'Sure hope not.' Jeff patted his saddle-bags before he lifted on to the horse's back. 'Another reason for getting there fast though,' he said. 'Feel better once Nate's got this stuff in his hands.'

He stared towards the dim line that was the distant mountains; a while ago he'd thought he heard an echo of thunder and now the sky had a red tinge, as if blood had already been spilt at Hell's Gate. Jeff suppressed a shiver, telling himself it was only his mind playing tricks; he was getting morbid. He'd be fine once he got the whiskey out of his system. The thought of liquor weighed heavy and he cursed inwardly; some day Rupe Krantz would pay dear for those two bottles.

★   ★   ★

Nate Grundy slid his foot forward a few inches. Somewhere behind him he guessed Joe Detelli was doing the same, but he could neither hear nor see the gambler. They were under the great stone arch of Hell's Gate and since he'd ordered the men to extinguish the fire the darkness was total. They were in luck, a thin layer of cloud had obscured both the moon and the stars. Nate paused and listened, just as he had a dozen times before; if Cord had a lookout posted the man was keeping real quiet.

He felt Joe at his elbow and moved on again. It had been a good choice. If any of them had a chance of making it undetected then Detelli was the man; he was small and light on his feet, silent as a shadow. Nate spared a brief thought for the men he'd sent to the top of the ridge. Out in the open there might be a little more light; he hoped Darbo was keeping a good watch. And that the man would obey orders.

Taking a couple more steps, his hand outstretched to keep in touch with the canyon wall, Nate felt the change in direction. Any second now they would be around the corner and out of sight of Hell's Gate. In daylight it would be suicide to pass through here, open as it was to crossfire from the heights on either side. If his plan worked he and Detelli would get clear before full daylight. If they didn't . . . He pushed the thought aside and went on, feeling carefully for each step, intent on keeping silent.

The darkness was total. Nate had never thought about how it felt to be blind; he hadn't expected to find it so difficult to keep his bearings. When the rock-face suddenly vanished from beneath his hand Nate stumbled, barely keeping his balance. He had known this moment must come but he was still unprepared for it. They'd chosen to follow the southern wall because it was unbroken until it reached this point, but now they had to strike out to the other side of the canyon and find the base of the pinnacle.

A hand reached, groping until it found his shoulder. He half turned, but he could see nothing of Detelli; they had dirtied their faces, finding black mud in the little pool beneath the waterfall. He raised one hand and held the gambler's fingers in place on his shoulder as he moved on, linking them. Nate kept the other hand stretched before him, questing in the darkness, as each of his feet slid forwards a few inches at a time. He had to get this right or they could find themselves going round in circles, hopelessly lost.

Nate breathed a silent sigh of relief when his fingers touched rock again. He lifted Detelli's hand from his shoulder and guided it to the wall of the canyon, hearing the tiniest grunt of approval from the little man. They skirted the base of the pinnacle. Nate could imagine the great spire of stone standing tall above the ridge and hoped Darbo and the other two men were keeping watch somewhere up there.

From now on Nate had only the brief glimpse he'd gained a week before to guide him. He tried to picture the deep bowl hollowed out of the mountains. They had to work their way deeper into the canyon, going up over an area of rough ground to the level shelf. A tumble of boulders had been flung down from the heights over the years. Some of them were slick with moss, for no sun ever penetrated here, and there were deep holes between the stones, waiting to trap a foot if a man got careless.

Over to the centre of the hollow the going would be easier; Nate peered into the night. Was he imagining that faint ribbon of lighter darkness? A narrow sandy trail led up to the caves pock-marking the sides of the bowl, that might be what he could see, but he wouldn't risk using it. There, if anywhere, the outlaws were likely to have posted a guard.

Detelli was right behind him; the man was like a ghost, a thing of no substance. They crept forward, sometimes feeling the way with their hands, crouching or going on all fours. They tried to keep close to the bottom of the cliff, but often huge boulders or slides of loose stone forced them to abandon it.

Despite Nate's care his boot slipped and his foot jammed down between two rocks. He felt wildly for a handhold, ripping skin off his fingers. He didn't fall far, but his leg was wrenched sideways, twisting his ankle so bad that the breath whistled from his lungs.

He clenched his teeth and stayed still, fighting the pain. It seemed like half a lifetime as he held his breath and waited for a light to appear above, for angry voices and the metallic sound of guns being cocked.

Nothing stirred. Wincing with the pain in his leg, Nate edged into motion once more, aiming to get back to the comparative shelter offered by the rock-face.

Shattering the silence, a rasping sound came from somewhere quite close, and again he was instantly still. A flame flared in the dark, then the match was shaken out and the glow of a cigarette took its place. There was a guard, and he was right in their path.

For long slow seconds Nate did nothing but breathe as slow and shallow as he could, watching as the tiny light brightened and dimmed. Then, with one more cautious heave, he located the canyon wall. He sagged against it, allowing himself to recognize that he was in trouble. Putting weight on his damaged leg caused terrible pain, and it was getting worse at every step. He wouldn't be leaving Hell's Gate on his feet.

Above the two crouching men, the end of the cigarette glowed as the lookout drew on it, then abruptly the pinpoint of red swung out over their heads as it was tossed away. The quiet tread of feet echoed back from the sides of the canyon. The guard was leaving.

Nate stared towards the receding footsteps, then he realized he could see the man, just the faintest outline of a figure. The sky was no longer black, it was a deep dark blue. Dawn wasn't far away, they had taken far too long.

There was no time to waste. The faintest sound of cloth brushing against stone told him Detelli was still following. Drawing blood as he bit down on his lip, Nate took a step, and another. He clamped down on a whimper, clutching at the rock-face for support.

The light was growing by the second. Detelli's hand was suddenly on his arm, for there was more noise, a rustling, the slow out-blowing of a breath. Nate shuddered as he took his weight on his injured leg and lowered his hand to grip the .45 at his side.

'Horses!' Detelli's voice was a low mumble, right beside Nate's ear.

There was a snort, then the stamp of a hoof. Falling to his hands and knees, Nate struggled over the last boulder. Joe Detelli, light on his feet as a girl and totally silent, went past him. By the time Nate pulled himself upright Detelli had untied the first two horses and was moving on down the line.

Nate stared at the shadowy shapes, confused. Eli had sworn they'd followed four horses to Hell's Gate, and there'd been no chance of anyone else riding in, yet there were five animals here.

Detelli was at the end of the line. Then disaster struck. The last horse, maybe a grey or sorrel, showed pale against the black cliff. It reared away from Detelli, neighing shrilly. The little man made a grab for the rein but the animal was already running, its feet noisy on the rock. Catching its fear, the rest of the horses turned too, heads high and eyes wild. 'Hey!' A voice shouted from the direction of the cave. 'What's goin' on down there? Mac, that you?'

Detelli had somehow got himself astride one of the horses. 'Here!' He was struggling to hold on to another, but the animal was fighting to get loose, tugging the rein through his fingers. Nate threw himself at the dim shape. Pain flared as his injured foot kicked back hard against the ground; he tried to twist around and get a leg over the horse's back, but his strength had deserted him.

Nate lay with the animal's backbone digging into his belly, twining his fingers desperately into its mane. 'Don't let go,' he gasped. Detelli cursed, fighting to keep his seat as the horses tried to pull apart.

13

The trail leading back to Hell's Gate was a dusky grey ribbon in a black landscape. Detelli reached it and jerked his horse's head around, urging it wildly downhill. Bouncing, sliding, in danger of having his brains dashed out on a rock at any second, Nate hung on as his own mount plunged on the end of the rein Detelli held, the horse trying to break free at every jarring stride.

The crack of a rifle shot split the air, then another and another, followed by a long rolling echo that thundered around the two fleeing men. Light was beginning to spill down from the brightening sky; they were visible.

More guns were firing now, but from the sound Nate knew they had to come from the ridge. So Darbo was awake! There was an exchange of shots; the attack from above was drawing the

185

outlaw's fire. They might still have a chance. He gritted his teeth and hung on.

A scream, pitched so high it hurt the ears, drowned out the sound of gunfire. It became an unearthly howl as it reverberated around the great rocky bowl, then it was abruptly cut off, leaving nothing but the last dying echo, like the memory of an evil dream.

After that no more shots sounded from the ridge. A hail of rifle fire shattered the brief silence, bullets ricocheting off the canyon wall beside the two riders. The horses balked, veering away from the lethal splinters of rock scything through the air.

Joe Detelli swore. He clamped his legs around the horse's ribs, sliding sideways, only desperation keeping him on its bare back as Nate's horse made one last bid to escape. The rein burned as it sliced between his fingers, then it was gone. Detelli hauled himself upright, clapping frantic heels against the animal's sides, lying low on its neck and aiming its nose at Hell's Gate. He could do no more for the sheriff, only hope that the horse would follow.

Nate's horse was free, bucking and plunging, the rein dangling round its front feet. There was light enough to see Hell's Gate now, the very top of the archway dark against the eastern sky. It looked impossibly distant.

A bullet whined past the horse's nose and it threw up its head in terror, swivelling on the spot, ready to gallop back the way it had come. Nate made a lunge for the trailing rein. Missing it, he had no alternative but to fling himself off the animal's back, curling into a defensive ball and feeling a glancing blow on his shoulder as a hoof caught him. Detelli's mount was flying towards Hell's Gate, the little man crouched low on its back.

Nate was out in the open, in the deadly killing ground where no help could reach him. Even with no hope of survival he wasn't ready to lie still and wait for a bullet. Unable to run since his ankle wouldn't bear his weight, he rolled, throwing himself over and over, slugs spitting up the dust around him. Somehow his eyes and brain made sense of the whirling landscape as he rolled. There was a shallow outcrop standing away from the rock-wall; reach that and he'd be under cover.

He was only a yard from comparative safety, though he'd still be the wrong side of Hell's Gate. Something hit him solidly in the back and knocked him flat. As his body absorbed the shock, Nate put his hands to the ground, heaving himself halfway up, getting his one good foot under him and lunging forward. The ground came leaping to meet him; the world exploded, bright with pain, then it faded into a welcoming blackness.

★   ★   ★

Since they'd broken camp at first light Jeff hadn't spoken a word to Cassie. The rhythmic hoofbeats told him the black mare was still behind him, the sound like an echo of the pain pounding through his head. He kept his eyes facing forward, squinting at the brightness of the day, now and then dragging the brim of his hat even lower over his eyes. The reins were gripped so tight in his left fist that every muscle in his arm was stiff and sore, while his right hand was clenched on the saddle bow. No matter how hard he held on, he could still feel the tremors rippling through his body.

The need for liquor was a constant scourge. He was almost grateful to be distracted by the punishment Rupe had meted out, but no amount of aches and bruises would have been enough. As the sun rose clear of the horizon, Jeff had to fight the temptation to turn the horse around and head back to Redemption. His gaze was fixed on the ground, following the tracks the posse had left the day before, but he hardly noticed them, locked as he was into his own private struggle.

'Is that the way into the canyons?'

Cassie's voice broke the silence and Jeff started. He'd almost forgotten she was there. The black mare came alongside, its rider leaning towards him, her face giving nothing away as she looked into his.

'What?' His tongue was dry and swollen. It hurt to talk. Without another word Cassie unslung her canteen and passed it over. Jeff drank deep. He resisted his stomach's attempt to throw the water straight up again, and by an effort of will he chased the thought of whiskey to the back of his mind.

'We must be almost there,' Cassie said.

'A mile I'd guess. We take the left fork here.' He pointed at the hoof marks in the dust. 'Come on.' The two horses jogged on, matching step for step. Jeff glanced side-long at his companion as they rode; the promises they'd made a couple of days ago seemed no more than a dream. The drink-sodden nightmare that Rupe had inflicted on him lay between them, harder to cross than any mountain range.

The posse was camped alongside a waterfall. The canyon's high wall offered shade from the midday sun. A bunch of horses stood close to the trickling fall of water, heads down and listless. As the two riders approached, a man came from amongst them.

'Jeff?' It was Jim Ormond, Redemption's blacksmith. 'What are you doing out here?'

Before Jeff could reply a tall skinny figure pushed up from beside the fire a little further on.

'You're kinda late,' Darbo grated, advancing on them. 'Ain't no place for you here.' He turned to Ormond. 'He got himself sworn in as a deputy the night before we left Redemption. Only he didn't turn up next day. Seems he preferred to crawl into a whiskey bottle.'

'I'm looking for Nate,' Jeff told the blacksmith, ignoring Darbo.

'The liquor gone to your ears? I said you ain't welcome.' Darbo caught hold of Jeff's horse by the bit and pulled it around, stopping in his tracks as he realized the second rider was a woman. 'Guess you're still drunk, else you're crazy, bringin' a woman out here.'

Jeff looked down into the small dark eyes, then with slow deliberation he lit down, to stand toe to toe with the taller man. 'I'm here to see the sheriff,' he said, taking each word clear and slow as if talking to an imbecile. 'How about you tell me where to find him?'

Darbo's mouth twisted. 'He's dead,' he said, 'or next thing to it.'

Jeff snapped around, taking in the faces of the men sitting by the fire. Joe Detelli was biting on his lip, his saloon pallor almost green in the deep shade. Shorty Sims gave Jeff a brief nod, a glum expression on his homely face.

'We don't know that for certain,' Jim Ormond said. 'Sure wish you'd been here earlier, Jeff. Reckon it's true what the marshal says though, it's too late now.'

'You want to tell me what the hell you're all talking about? And where's Eli? Something happen to him too?'

'I'm right here.' The old man came from deeper into the canyon, a rifle hanging loose in his hand. He stopped and looked Jeff up and down from ten yards away, his eyes hostile. 'Hate to say it, but Marshal Darbo's got it right. You let the boy down, Jeff, an' he's payin' high for it.'

'He didn't . . . ' Cassie Hanson began, but Jeff silenced her with a look.

'Later,' he said. 'You saying Nate's hurt? Where is he?'

'Come take a look,' Eli turned on his heel. Jeff Warrinder glanced at Jim, who shrugged. Joe Detelli refused to meet his eyes.

'He's got no business here,' Darbo called after them, as Jeff hurried to catch up with the old man.

'We're goin' in there,' Eli said,

pointing. 'An' keep your head down,' he added gruffly.

Jeff crawled under the great archway after the old man, hugging the rock wall. Herb Ormond lay on his stomach at the end of the deep shadow, a rifle in his hand.

'Howdy, Jeff,' he said, acknowledging the new arrival with a nod of his head. 'It don't look good, Eli. Nobody's tried nothin', but he ain't moved.'

Eli turned to Jeff. 'He had this idea. Him an' Joe was tryin' — '

'How he got there doesn't matter. You know how bad he's hurt?' Jeff demanded, staring at the man who lay sprawled in the dust about twenty yards away. The sun had moved around so it beat down on the shock of tow-coloured hair.

'Joe didn't see. Bullet took him in the back, and that puddle of blood's gettin' bigger.'

'While he's bleeding he's still alive.' Jeff slithered backwards, getting to his feet once he was clear and hurrying

194

back towards the camp, with Eli almost trotting to keep up. 'But we need to get him out, and fast.'

'Tarnation, you think we don't know that! There's four men with rifles up there, just waitin' for us to try.'

'Then we'd best make sure they don't see us. What are you burning on that fire?'

'Jim dragged in a dead tree. An' there's plenty of dry cattle shit.'

'Then get some of it up here. Only we'll need something damp as well, something that'll make smoke.'

Darbo was waiting by the camp-fire, a scowl on his face and a Winchester repeater in his hands. 'I told you to go, Warrinder. Now Grundy's gone I'm the law here . . . '

'I know how to get Nate out,' Jeff said, cutting across the marshal's words. He realized his hands were shaking, and he clenched them into fists.

'It can't be done. The sheriff knew what he was riskin'. We already lost two men up on the ridge this mornin'.' Darbo's lip curled in contempt. 'Grundy wouldn't expect us to risk any more lives on some crazy stunt cooked up by the town drunk. Look at yourself, Warrinder, you're no lawman, not even a two-dollars-a-day deputy.'

Jeff flexed his shoulders and took a deep breath, resisting the temptation to take a swing at the man's face. 'You're right,' he said. 'I'm not here as a lawman. I'm here as a friend of Nate's. Seems like he needs one. Shorty, Jim, Joe, we have to make ourselves some smoke.'

* * *

Joe Detelli rode through the camp with a bandanna tied tight over his nose and mouth. A cloud of flies buzzed angrily over the black shapeless lump he was dragging at the end of a rope, and a sickening stench filled the space between the canyon walls.

'Can't have been dead more than two

days,' he said, helping Shorty Sims to heave the steer's rotting carcass onto the heap of wood that blazed at the entrance to Hell's Gate. 'Should smoke some.' He went to join Jeff who stood at the side of the arch, staring through at the path beyond. 'I sure hope he's still alive. Jeff, I didn't want to run out on him . . . '

Jeff clapped a hand on the gambler's shoulder. 'If you hadn't you'd be lying alongside him, dead maybe. Wasn't a bad idea trying to sneak their horses out of there, and you came close.'

Detelli shrugged. 'Close don't win no chips. I didn't see what happened once the horse pulled away. When I look again Nate's down. He hurt his foot; guess that's why he couldn't get himself on the critter's back.'

'You know what happened to Louis? Eli didn't say, just that him and Darbo and Kemp were supposed to be giving you some cover if you needed it.'

'Darbo says Louis got hit, took a slug to the chest. Kemp, he went to see if he could help, only he got too near the edge. He slipped and fell, all the way to the bottom.' He shuddered. 'We heard a scream. Not that we knew what it was. Far as I could tell Darbo didn't shoot no more. He said he went to Louis, found he was dead, and by that time wasn't anything he could do to help Nate.'

'Sounds like somebody in there is real good with a rifle, to pick Louis off that way.'

'Yeah. And Nate. Even though he couldn't walk he was a pretty fast-moving target. Eli was waiting under here, but he couldn't see nothing to shoot at.'

'Hey, Jeff, this what you want?' Shorty Sims yelled. He was fanning the fire with a blanket, and a pall of black smoke was rolling into Hell's Gate.

14

Every surviving member of the posse, except Darbo, volunteered to go through Hell's Gate with Jeff Warrinder.

'Not you, Eli,' Jeff said. 'We'll likely have to move fast.'

'But I could give you cover. Suppose I just come a little ways . . . '

'Forget it. If we start shooting we'll just give 'em something to aim at. Shorty's coming because he's the biggest, reckon he can carry Nate on his own if needs be. The rest of you, keep the smoke coming, or they'll be picking us off like fish in a barrel.'

Shorty followed Jeff in under the towering archway. High up the smoke clung to the roof, but it was thinner low down, drifting around their heads in grey wisps that stank with a mix of rotten flesh and scorched meat.

Jim Ormond had taken Herb's place.

Under cover of the haze he crawled a little closer to the bright patch of sunlight. He stared along the sights of his rifle.

'Reckon they can't see so good . . . ' he began. The crack of a gunshot cut him short. His rifle fell in the dust and he slid back into the shadows, his left hand cradled in his right. 'All right?' Jeff asked.

'Dammit! That hurt! I never saw nobody that good with a rifle. Look at that.' He held up his hand to show that the top half-inch of his index finger was missing. Blood was oozing from the wound.

'Get back to the camp and let Eli tend it. No point staying, we don't want to draw their fire.' Jeff glanced back past his boots. Beneath an approaching roll of smoke he could see three pairs of legs; the men looked like they were performing a frantic hoe-down as they fanned the blaze.

'Ready, Shorty? When the smoke reaches us we go with it.' The smoke came rolling over them, thick enough to choke on. The two men edged forward with fumes billowing around them.

'Didn't think about this,' Shorty said, coughing as he stumbled alongside Jeff. 'Them outlaws ain't the only ones who can't see, an' I can't breathe too good neither.'

Trying to breathe shallow, Jeff said nothing, concentrating on keeping a straight course to where he knew Nate lay. Shorty coughed again and something whistled past, hitting the canyon wall with an angry spitting sound.

'Hush up,' Jeff whispered. 'Move fast and stay low.' He put his head down and ran. Two more rifles barked, but the shots came nowhere near. Nate had to be just ahead. Jeff pulled up just short of crashing headfirst into the cliff. Only a yard away the outcrop jutted from the rock face, and he fell to his knees at Nate Grundy's side.

'Down,' he said, grabbing Shorty by the arm and pulling the big man into cover.

The reeking clouds eddied round the little hollow. Jeff couldn't see; his eyes were stinging and running with water. He rubbed at them. 'Nate?'

'Jeff? That you?' The voice was thin with pain. 'What in all the halls of hell are you doing here?'

'We'll chew that over once we get you out,' Jeff said quietly. He scowled down at his friend. The back of his shirt was black with blood, but the bullet had struck high; if it had hit anything vital Nate would surely have been dead by now.

'Can't walk,' Nate said, trying to lift himself on his hands. 'Bust my ankle.'

'We'll do the walking,' Jeff replied. 'But it'll hurt some. Reckon you can keep your mouth shut? There's a man out there with a rifle; we mustn't give him anything to aim at.'

'You get me out of here and I swear I won't say a word for a week,' Nate said feebly.

Jeff nodded. 'A couple of minutes'll do it. Here, Shorty.' They lifted him between them. Nate's back arched in pain, but he made no sound.

'Which way?' Shorty whispered, staring around in confusion.

'Into the wind,' Jeff replied. 'Fast as you can. But keep your head down.'

The outlaws seemed to have guessed their intentions. Rifle fire ripped through the smoke above the two men's heads as they carried their burden back across the open ground towards the archway. The air was alive with flying lead. With that amount of fire being poured down on them it seemed only a matter of seconds before one of them got hit.

Half seeing the figures of men before him in the grey gloom Jeff's heart lurched, but it was only Herb and Eli. The two men were walking backwards and as they retreated they opened fire; their intervention seemed to deter Cord and his men, for only a smattering of bullets followed as Jeff and Shorty carried the sheriff through Hell's Gate to safety.

By the time Nate had been laid down

in the shade Cassie Hanson was there beside him. She had a bundle of white cloth in her hands and, as she met Jeff's eyes above the injured man, she flushed a little. 'Girl can't even hold onto her shirt,' she said. 'We'll need some water heating on that fire.'

'I'll get it,' Herb Ormond trotted off down the canyon.

'Wouldn't it be better to take him back to the camp?' Jeff asked, doubled over against the cliff as he tried to catch his breath, his voice rasping with the effects of the smoke. 'It'll only take us a couple of minutes.'

'You'll have done enough damage bringing him this far. Eli, give me a hand here.'

Jeff looked at the group of men gathered round them. 'Anybody got any liquor?' He caught the sharp glances that scorched between Cassie and old Eli.

Joe Detelli reached inside his vest. 'Whiskey.' He pulled out a flask. 'Not much left, but I've got a bottle back at the camp.'

'Give it to Mrs Hanson,' Jeff said roughly, turning to look at Cassie. 'Best thing for cleaning a wound. Anything else you need?'

She shook her head. 'If me and Eli can't manage I'll call.'

'Hold it,' Nate whispered, gesturing feebly. 'Jeff, that night, before we left town. You said you'd got a plan . . . Cord . . . And Brodie . . . Least we got ten of us now you're here, but there's morc'n three men in there..'

'I know it. Don't you fret,' Jeff told him. He grimaced; his friend hadn't heard yet that they'd lost Louis Jardine and Deputy Kemp. 'We'll get 'em, Nate. Just make sure you're fit to be at the hanging.'

* * *

A couple of hours later, Jeff Warrinder followed Shorty Sims along the ridge, slow across the rough ground.

'Near that stone spike,' Shorty said. 'Darbo reckoned he buried him good, just where he died, but a man needs a friend to see it's done right.'

'There.' Jeff pointed. A few rocks had been piled together, but a pair of boots stuck out from beneath them. 'It looks as if the marshal was in a hurry.'

'Tarnation, you got that right!' Shorty Sims snorted. 'Was up here long enough.'

He began to gather more stones, but Jeff knelt by the grave to remove the ones Darbo had used, and in a short time he was lifting the blanket that covered Louis Jardine's body.

'Hey!' Shorty was indignant. 'What you doin'?'

'Darbo lied about giving Louis a decent burial. I wonder if he told the truth about the way he died.'

There wasn't much blood. Jeff pulled Jardine's shirt open to take a closer look at the gunshot wound. He could see nothing that didn't tie in with Darbo's story. They knew one of the outlaws was pretty smart with a rifle; young Monty had died the same way.

'Where's his vest?' Shorty said suddenly.

'You sure he was wearing one?'

'Yeah. Joe joshed him about it. It was fancy, kinda silvery, with red stitchin'.'

Jeff thought about it. Why would Darbo take a ruined vest? He eased the corpse on to its side. 'There,' he said.

Shorty pulled the bloodstained garment from beneath Jardine's body. 'Why'd he do that?'

Jeff didn't answer, taking the vest. He looked at the bullet hole. A little blood rimmed it. And a few tiny black marks. Powder burns? But with the shot fired from over twenty yards away that couldn't be.

'You can cover him up again,' he said.

Careful to keep low, Jeff went looking for the place where Deputy Kemp had lost his footing and fallen to his death. If he'd been hurrying to help Jardine he couldn't have been too far from this spot when he slipped. There was a chance he'd have left some sign, scuff marks perhaps. Jeff found nothing until he was more than ten yards from the grave. Several dark spots that looked like dried blood stained the top of a boulder. He raked at the dust with his fingers and found more.

'Somethin' wrong?' Shorty asked, coming to look for him.

'Maybe.' Jeff shrugged. 'Come on, if you're done I need to talk to Nate.'

An hour later Jeff was lowering himself down the rope alongside the waterfall. He felt like hell. His mouth was dry as dust and his head was pounding.

'Hey, somebody's comin'.' Shorty pointed to the mouth of the canyon. There were three riders, the one in front mounted on a big chestnut. Jeff squeezed his aching eyes shut. The thought of a confrontation with Rupe Krantz didn't appeal right now.

Herb Ormond was filling a bucket at the bottom of the falls, and he walked back to camp with them. They found Rupe hunkered down by the fire, talking intently to Darbo. He stood up and smiled broadly as Jeff approached.

'Well, look who's here. Just been telling the marshal how you lit out of town so suddenly. And how you took my little lady along.'

Jeff glanced at Darbo. There was a leering contempt on the marshal's thin face. 'Your little lady?' Jeff drawled. 'Mrs Hanson wouldn't touch you with a ten-foot pole.'

Across the camp-fire the two Double Bar K hands rose to their feet. Neither of them looked much like a cowboy. One was a beefy mean-faced man by the name of Hanks, well known in Redemption as a dirty fighter; it had been Hanks's hand almost throttling Jeff a couple of nights ago while Rupe poured whiskey down his throat.

The other man wore a fancy black-handled six-gun tied low on his hip. It was said Morrissey had once ridden with the James' gang, though as far as Jeff knew there'd never been a warrant out on him.

Herb Ormond looked uneasily from

Jeff to the three newcomers. 'We got enough trouble here with a handful of outlaws. No call to fight among ourselves.'

Shorty Sims stepped up alongside Jeff, a smile on his face. 'Mrs Hanson, she's Jeff's girl. They come ridin' in together this mornin'.' The big hands were curling into fists as he spoke, and Jeff wondered if the man had more sense than folks gave him credit for.

'Now that can't be.' Rupe's own smile didn't waver. 'Cassie's agreed to be Mrs Krantz. I won't deny we had a disagreement a while back, but I'm here to see that's all smoothed over. If you'll just tell me where I'll find her then we'll be on our way.'

'Over my dead body,' Jeff growled, keeping a wary eye on Morrissey's hand as it crept towards the ebony gun-butt at his side.

'If that's the way you want it,' Rupe said smoothly.

'Hold it, Warrinder.' Marshal Darbo stepped between them.

'Like I said, Marshal, he hasn't been sober in years,' Rupe said. 'Ask Sheriff Grundy. Only time he's not rolling drunk is when he's sleeping it off in jail. You can't believe Mrs Hanson came along willingly; no decent woman would be seen with such a bum.'

'That's enough,' Jeff's voice was dangerously quiet.

'It's a private fight, Marshal,' Morrissey said. 'Ain't a matter for the law.'

'Maybe you're right.' Darbo nodded. 'I already told you to get out of here, Warrinder. Walk away now and you ain't gonna come to no harm.'

'I see no reason to leave,' Jeff said evenly.

Darbo shrugged. 'Suit yourself. Figure I'll take a ride, we'll be needin' more wood for the fire.' He turned and left, not giving Jeff another glance.

'Hey, Marshal.' Shorty spun around as if to go after the lawman, his open features creased by an unaccustomed frown. 'What about — ?'

Hanks's fist caught the big man hard

above the ear, and Shorty crashed to the ground like a felled tree. Darbo must have heard but he gave no sign of it, keeping his back to them until he reached the horses.

With his hand still hovering over his holster, Morrissey set his gaze on Herb Ormond, showing discoloured teeth in an evil grin. 'Reckon you got better things to do, mister,' he said. 'Why don't you take a walk?'

Herb gave Jeff a worried glance.

'It's all right, Herb.' Jeff jerked his head towards Hell's Gate. 'Go ahead. But if I was you I wouldn't turn my back till I was out of range.'

Obediently Ormond eased away, not taking his eyes off them until he was out of pistol shot, then spinning around and breaking into a run as he reached the bend in the canyon wall.

Rupe laughed. 'Just you and me, Warrinder.'

'Well sure,' Jeff replied, 'so long as you don't count the hired help. Face it, Rupe, you'll never have the guts to take me on your own. What's it to be, a bullet in the back from Morrissey while you and Hanks keep me entertained?'

The other man's face darkened. 'I don't need them. I can — '

Jeff had been ready for Morrissey's move. As the man's gun cleared the holster his right hand came up holding the .32 Cassie had given him, his left coming across as he fired, ready to fan back the hammer. Morrissey squeezed the trigger of his .45 Colt, turning as he did so, sacrificing accuracy in an attempt to reduce Jeff's chances of hitting him. The sudden move spoiled his shot and the bullet went wide. Jeff's first slug sliced across Morrissey's ribs. It didn't do much damage but it was enough to slow the man down, the shock of the impact making him pull back.

Before the gunman could recover, Jeff's second shot took him in the throat. As he fell, Morrissey's fingers clenched convulsively and the .45 spat another slug into the dust at Rupe's feet.

Hanks hadn't waited to see if Morrissey won the battle. As he realized the danger, Jeff began to move but it was already too late. The same great fist that had felled Shorty came slamming into the side of his head. If he'd been standing still the punch would have knocked him cold, but he'd been shifting his weight and he kept his feet somehow, staggering sideways under the blow, with the world spinning around him.

Something solid struck the .32 from Jeff's hand; Rupe had seen his chance and taken it, bringing the butt of his six-gun sweeping down. Instinct kept Jeff moving though he could barely see, but he misjudged and blundered dazedly against the surly Hanks, who thudded a ham-sized fist into his kidneys. Jeff went down hard. Knowing Hanks of old, he twisted to keep himself clear of the man's feet, only to get a sharp kick to the head from Rupe.

If Jeff was to survive he had to get back to his feet. He put his hands to the ground, though he hardly knew which way was up. He heard the distinctive sound of metal on metal as a gun was cocked.

'That has to be a new low, Rupe, even for you, shooting a helpless man.' Cassie's voice shook but it rang out loud and clear. 'Getting your men to beat him up and forcing whiskey down his throat was cowardly enough, but this takes the biscuit.'

15

Jeff squeezed his eyelids down hard and when he opened them he could see Cassie, though his sight was clouded by a red haze of pain. There were other figures further back, but he couldn't bring them into focus.

'Well?' she said, breaking a long silence, her gaze fixed steadily on some point behind Jeff's head. 'Are you ready to commit murder?'

'It wouldn't be murder,' Rupe said, his voice husky. From where he lay Jeff couldn't see the man's face, but his tone spoke his feelings; Jeff's life hung on a thread. Rupe had his enemy at his feet, and he wanted to finish what he'd started. 'He killed Morrissey.'

'In self-defence.' Herb Ormond said, stepping forward to join the woman. 'We saw it. Put away the gun, Krantz.'

In the pause that followed, Jeff

levered himself to his knees. The six-gun Rupe had knocked from his hand lay out of reach and for the moment he made no move towards it. He watched Rupe's shadow, motionless on the ground beside his own.

'I'll let him go on one condition,' Rupe said at last. 'You and me have a talk, Cassie. A private talk. I figure you haven't given me a fair hearing. It's time we got things straightened out.'

'All right,' said Cassie.

'No,' Jeff growled, getting a foot to the ground and coming up slowly, not trusting his balance. He eased around so he could see Rupe Krantz.

The woman ignored him. 'Put the gun away and I'll walk over to the horse line with you. Mr Warrinder won't interfere. And tell that tame grizzly of yours to behave himself.'

'You sure this is what you want, ma'am?' It was Eli's voice. Jeff hadn't known the old man was there.

'Yes.' She was adamant. 'Rupe?'

His eyes still on Jeff and full of

loathing, Rupe Krantz uncocked the gun and slid it back into its holster. 'Hanks, you stay here.' He jerked his head towards Morrissey. 'Get a hole dug. And keep your hands off Warrinder until I get back.'

Jeff took a step towards Cassie as if to stop her. 'You don't have to do this,' he said.

She glared at him. 'I know.' There was a coldness in her eyes he'd never seen there before, not even that first day by the river. It stopped him in his tracks. She turned and walked away with Rupe Krantz. Jeff stayed where he was, though his every instinct told him to follow them.

Shorty Sims stirred and groaned, the sound breaking into the charged silence. Herb went to him, while Jeff stepped across to look down at Morrissey, careful not to move too fast. The man lay in a gory pool, staring sightlessly up at the canyon wall; it had taken him only seconds to bleed to death. Jeff stooped to pick up his gun. He met Hanks's eyes briefly. 'You'll find a shovel by the fire,' he said. Hanks gave a slight shrug and went to fetch it.

'Won't be enough of this posse left to take on Cord and Brodie,' Eli said drily, coming to Jeff's side. 'Shame Rupe didn't bring a few more of his sidekicks.'

'Since when did the Krantz family ever do anything to uphold the law?' Jeff asked bitterly. 'You really think Rupe and his boys came out here to get themselves sworn in as deputies?'

'I'd guess they came lookin' for you.'

'And Mrs Hanson. Bull Krantz has got his eyes on the Lazy Zee, and he figures Rupe's the one to get it for him.' Jeff kept his eyes on the two remote figures over by the horses. Cassie was absently stroking the black mare's nose, her head down as she listened to what Rupe had to say.

'How's Nate?' he asked abruptly, tearing his gaze away.

'He got lucky. Bullet wasn't too deep. It must've been nigh on spent by the time it hit him. But his ankle's bad, he's gonna be off his feet quite a while.' The wrinkles on Eli's face deepened. 'Guess you done your best to put things right, but you didn't oughta let him down that way. You shoulda ridden with the posse, Jeff. Nobody blamed you for takin' to whiskey when Sarah died, but the longer a man keeps climbin' into the bottle the harder it gets to pull hisself out again.'

'I didn't . . . ' Jeff began, then broke off as Cassie stepped away from Rupe and started back towards them. She looked small and very much alone. He wanted to run and take her in his arms, but common sense told him that while his head kept spinning he'd more likely fall at her feet.

'I have something to say.' Her face was grave but composed. 'No, don't go,' she said, as Eli turned to leave. 'I want somebody else to hear this, so it's clear and out in the open.'

'Cassie — '

'Wait, Jeff.' She looked up to meet his

eyes. 'You have to hear me out, please. I didn't tell you the whole truth about me and Rupe. It was true he'd been to see me at the Lazy Zee a time or two. And I didn't run him off.'

A flush rose from her neck to give her pale cheeks a pink glow. 'We were about ready to come to an agreement. I won't spell it out, you know what I mean. But then we had an argument, and I told him never to come near me again.' Cassie Hanson's voice faltered and she dropped her gaze. 'That's why Bull dragged me off to jail. He said I'd gone back on my word. It was supposed to teach me a lesson.

'I was furious with Rupe. With both of them. That's why I took you to the Lazy Zee, and made you work for me. I never meant . . . once you'd got the liquor out of your system you were so kind to me. I could see what you were thinking. I didn't know how to put things right. It was all a terrible mistake. I never should have let it go on . . . '

'I don't believe this,' Jeff said thickly, clenching his fists. 'What was Rupe saying to you just now? Did he threaten you?' He looked over towards the horses but nobody was there.

'No!' She met his look again and her eyes were damp. 'He's keeping out of it, so you know this comes from me, not him.'

'We both made a promise. You can't tell me you didn't mean it.' He put out a hand to her but she backed away.

'Please, let me say my piece. I made a mistake and I'm sorry. I believe you're a good and honest man, Jeff. You really think you can change. I know Rupe forced that whiskey on you the other night, and I know you did all you could to fight him. But I'll never be able to forget what happened to my father. There were times when he struggled against it too. Once he stayed sober for a whole year; that was the happiest time I'd ever known, until I married Steve.

'Maybe you're a stronger man than my father,' she went on. 'Maybe you'll keep off the drink for ten years, or even twenty. But the temptation would always be there. I can't live through that again. I'm so sorry.'

'Have you promised yourself to Rupe Krantz?'

'Not yet. But I haven't turned him down.' There was a sudden flash of anger in her eyes. 'Maybe that matters more to you than I do. You hate Rupe so much you can't bear to see him take something you thought was yours.'

'You don't believe that.' There was no answering anger in him, only a bottomless despair. 'If I thought Rupe would make you happy . . . '

'What? You'd shake his hand and wish him good luck?' She shook her head hopelessly. 'I'm not asking you to do that. I never meant to hurt you, Jeff. I truly hope that you find somebody else, somebody who's worth staying sober for. Just say I'm forgiven. Ride back to Redemption and forget about me.'

★   ★   ★

In half an hour it would be dark. Jeff Warrinder kicked back with his heels as the horse slowed. There was foam on the animal's neck, and steam rose from its heaving flanks. He'd galloped all the way from the canyons, barely aware of his direction, urging his borrowed mount to run flat out for mile after mile. Now it stumbled and almost fell.

Some distant part of his mind told Jeff he couldn't go on pressing the poor beast so hard. It needed rest. He eased back and at once the horse slowed to a walk. Jeff looked around to gather his bearings. The horse was heading for home; another mile and they'd be at the water-hole where he and Cassie had spent the previous night. Lighting down, Jeff patted the hot wet neck by way of apology, cursing himself; when he was a lawman he'd never driven a horse so hard without need. But that was in another lifetime. He'd been a different man then, maybe the kind of man who deserved a woman like Cassie Hanson.

He led his weary mount that last mile. By the time they reached the water-hole night had come. Jeff tended to the horse, then he sat by the dead remains of their camp-fire and stared at the ashes, clenching and unclenching his fists. Images of the woman he loved spun around in his aching head; he could see her laughing up at him while he fixed the roof; he felt the tender touch of her lips on his.

Always his thoughts brought him back to the emptiness in her eyes as she'd sent him away. He tried to summon up a righteous fury at her betrayal, but there was no anger in him. He couldn't blame her for turning him down. She'd been right that first day when she'd called him a drunken bum. Groaning out loud, Jeff sank his head into his trembling hands; he'd brought nothing but harm to the two women he loved.

With an effort Jeff dragged his thoughts away from Sarah and Cassie, but that left him with only one thing on his mind. He needed a drink. He recalled that Joe Detelli had a bottle. Jeff hadn't an ounce of pride left but he couldn't go back to Hell's Gate. And Redemption was a hard day's ride away.

He pushed himself to his feet, easing movement into his cramped legs, then he set about rekindling the fire. The coffee he made was strong, but it had no taste. There was a darkness in his soul far blacker than the moonless night. He cursed Rupe Krantz for not pulling the trigger and putting an end to his misery.

At last Jeff slept, but he had no peace. He dreamt that Cassie Hanson leant over him, a bottle in her hand. 'Rupe wants you to have it,' she said, smiling. 'Because he's got me.' Then she disappeared and he was looking at Nate across the street outside his office; there was a hole in his throat with the blood pumping out. The young sheriff stared reproachfully at Jeff as he fell to the ground, a red froth bubbling from his mouth. Jeff ran to him, but when he got there he found himself looking down into Sarah's beautiful dead face.

'No!' Jeff's scream of protest woke him, and he struggled out of his bedroll, his head pounding. He fingered the place where Rupe had kicked him, feeling dried blood. That was the least of his ills. His whole body ached with the need for whiskey. Throwing more fuel on the fire he began to pace, striding from the fire to the edge of the water-hole and back again. With only a few fitful stars showing he couldn't guess how long he had to wait for the sunrise, but nightmares lay in wait and he daren't sleep again; he stayed on his feet, pausing only when he had to feed the dying fire, measuring out the endless night ten paces at a time.

The faint glimmer of dawn was showing in the east. Jeff Warrinder veered aside from the track he'd trampled in the dust and knelt to plunge his head and neck into the water, dousing himself over and over, rubbing hard at his scalp until blood ran from the wound inflicted by Rupe Krantz's boot. He was unutterably weary but his head was clear; there'd been plenty of time for thinking, and remembering. He knew what he had to do.

*   *   *

'Ain't no help for it.' Marshal Darbo pulled a brand from the fire to light a cigarette, drawing hard until its tip glowed red in the darkness 'Them four could stay holed up for a month or more, an' there's nothin' we can do, not without more men.'

'You shouldn't have let Jeff Warrinder go,' Nate Grundy said, looking up at him. He shifted, trying to ease the pain in his leg. 'He could have been useful.'

'That plan he told you about.' Darbo snorted. 'It weren't no more'n hot air. Maybe he was a decent lawman once, but there ain't no trustin' a drunk. He took to the bottle instead of ridin' with us. And he shot Krantz's man. Lucky for him Morrissey wasn't a deputy.'

Nate shook his head. 'I never knew the Krantzes to help the law, Rupe didn't come all the way out here to join the posse.'

'Just what he has done,' Darbo said. 'I swore him an' the other one in myself.'

'Hanks?' Nate looked at the marshal in disgust. 'He's not a man I'd choose to have on my side.'

'He'll do well enough. This ain't no place for a handful of townsfolk, Sheriff; you don't wanna risk losin' any more of your men. It took troops to shoehorn the Meacher gang out of Hell's Gate, an' that's what we're gonna need now.'

Nate nodded slowly. He felt so weary it was hard to think. 'Maybe. You say you know who's in there with Cord and the others?'

'Man by the name of Steiger, I reckon. I heard a rumour that him an' Brodie was the ones who robbed that train outside Denver last fall. Took 'emselves nigh on a hundred thousand dollars.'

'That's a good enough reason for the army to turn out. But we'll have to keep the canyon bottled up tight till they get here.'

'I know it,' Darbo said. 'But there'll be help comin' real soon. I happen to know there's a detachment of troops at Saquiro Rock. I sent Hanks with a message a couple of hours ago, they'll be here by tomorrow night.'

'You sound awful sure of it,' Nate said.

'Sure I'm sure. Their captain's an old friend. He'll come.' Darbo flung the cigarette butt into the fire. 'Nothin' more for you an' your men to do here, Sheriff. I told the old man to fix up a travois for you, seein' as you ain't fit to ride. You can all be on your way at first light.'

16

The light was growing. As Jeff carried
his saddle towards his borrowed horse
it stopped grazing, lifting its head to
stare to the north as if it heard
something. Silently easing the saddle to
the ground Jeff drew the ancient .32
Cassie Hanson had given him; he'd left
the shotgun with Eli, asking the old
man to return it to her.

He took a few steps into the deeper
shadows by a patch of juniper, out of
sight of the trail. Moments passed then
his horse gave a soft call of welcome
and the thud of hoofs could be heard
through the morning calm. Jeff knew
the little black mare's paces; the hope
that Cassie had followed him was
scarcely alive before it died.

Silence. The horse had stopped. Jeff
waited, ears stretched for the slightest
sound.

'Warrinder? You there?' It was Hanks.

The man dismounted, a heavy thud sounding as his feet hit the ground. Jeff crouched so he could see the man outlined against the sky, and make out the rifle in his hands. He cocked the .32, making no attempt to do it quietly.

'Lay down your gun or you're a dead man.'

'Warrinder? Hell, no need for that kinda talk. Figured I could share your fire awhile, an' maybe bum a cup of coffee. Been a long night. Never did care for ridin' when I can't see the trail; damn horse kept spookin'.' Hanks held the rifle out to his side at arm's length. 'Don't mean you no harm.'

'What are you doing here?'

'Just passin' through.'

'On your own? Where's Rupe?' Jeff asked.

'With the posse.' The man gave a humourless laugh. 'If he wants to risk his neck for two dollars a day that's his affair, but I ain't got no quarrel with them *hombres* in the canyon. I reckon

Rupe's only stayin' to impress the little lady. Fact is, I'm kinda partial to keepin' a whole skin.'

'Rupe didn't send you?'

'Send me? What, to track you down? Mister, I ain't that kinda fool. I seen what Morrissey got. Don't reckon there's no hard feelin's between you an' me.'

'No?' Jeff said wryly. 'You were pretty handy with your fists the other night; reckon I owe you a bruise or two.'

'When you work for the Double Bar K you do as you're told an' keep your mouth shut. If I hadn't beat up on you somebody else would. You know Rupe, he don't listen to nobody. Anyway I quit. I'm gonna pick up my pay from Bull then head south.' Hanks's eyes scanned the patch of juniper, his hands dropping a little. 'Sure could use a mouthful of coffee.'

'Put that gun on the ground. And your belt. Then you can help yourself.'

Hanks stared uneasily into the dense cover where Jeff stood then gave a slow nod, lowering the rifle to the dirt before unbuckling his gunbelt. 'You sure are one suspicious *hombre*.'

'I find it helps a man to stay alive.'

They sat either side of the fire, facing each other.

'That's good coffee,' Hanks said. 'Got somethin' in my bedroll that'll make it taste even better.' He half rose, his eyes on the .32 that was still in Jeff's hand. 'You got my guns, Sheriff.'

'I'm no more sheriff than you are,' Jeff replied. 'Go ahead, but do it slow.' He relaxed a little. There was plenty of light now, and Hanks wasn't a gunman, just hired muscle.

Hanks nodded. He went to his horse and untied his bedroll, coming back carrying a stone jar between his hands. 'Finest corn liquor north of the Arkansas. Wanna join me?'

Jeff swallowed, his throat constricting suddenly. He slid the .32 back into its holster, resisting the temptation to tear the jar from the other man's grasp.

Hanks drank deep. 'Sure beats that

stuff the Krantzes like.' He offered the jar to Jeff. As Jeff stretched to take it his hand shook uncontrollably; he pulled it back as if he'd been burned. 'Gets a man drunk just the same,' he said.

Hanks shrugged and took another pull, slopping a little of the liquor down the front of his shirt. 'Suit yourself.'

The smell was overpowering. 'Guess a mouthful won't do any harm,' Jeff said thickly.

With a grin Hanks leant forward to hand him the jar. 'Sure thing.'

For a mere speck of time the sun shone clear in the big man's eyes. Jeff looked into them and saw triumph, and contempt. He'd been right: Hanks wasn't here by chance. It seemed Rupe Krantz wasn't satisfied with taking Cassie Hanson, he wanted more.

Hanks must have seen the change in Jeff's expression; his own face grew suddenly ugly. Still holding the jar in his right hand, he lunged across the camp-fire to clamp his left around Jeff's wrist before he could draw the .32.

Heaving with all his considerable strength he dragged Jeff towards him, so his boots knocked the coffee pot over and scattered the fire. Twisting his wrist he swung Jeff down and around so his face was only inches above the hot embers.

Hanks put the jar on the ground. 'We're gonna need that,' he said, smiling. 'Don't matter how it goes down your throat; it's worth an extra two hundred bucks if the sheriff finds you drunk when the posse comes by.'

Jeff almost had his left hand to the butt of the .32, but Hanks was too quick, striking down with his fist, a numbing blow that sent Jeff's arm into the remnants of the fire. He bit down on a scream as his arm scorched, but he didn't instantly push up and away from the searing heat, forcing his fingers to obey him, feeling around in the hot dry dust even as the sickly smell of burnt flesh filled the air.

'Hell!' Hanks pulled him upright,

grinning widely. 'Don't want you roasted.'

His face contorting with pain, Jeff's hand came up bearing the half-burnt branch he'd grasped, its end glowing red. He stabbed wildly at Hanks.

A scream pierced the air. Jeff dropped and rolled as Hanks released him, his right hand reaching for the .32, his left arm a burning agony. Getting to his feet, Jeff skittered around the fire, scooping up the other man's gunbelt from the ground with his uninjured fingers. He kicked Hanks's rifle into the water-hole then plunged in after it.

Hanks came blundering into the water too, swearing and spluttering, his hands clawing at his face. Letting the cold water ease away the worst of the pain in his arm, Jeff kept the .32 trained on Hanks, but it seemed the Double Bar K man had other things on his mind.

Jeff climbed out first, pulling away the burnt ruins of his sleeve. It was bad enough; a strip of flesh from wrist to elbow was blistering, but he could still use his arm and his hand was barely damaged. His opponent hadn't been so lucky. When Hanks finally lifted his head out of the water his right eye socket glistened red and black. Jeff hadn't meant to blind him; the blow had been random, an act of desperation.

'Damn you!' Hanks gasped, struggling out of the water-hole and grabbing the jar of whiskey. He drank long and deep, pausing only to curse again.

'You didn't give me much choice,' Jeff said. 'Seems you won't be claiming that two hundred.'

'Rupe swore you'd be gaspin' for a drink,' Hanks said, his voice ragged with pain. He swallowed some more. 'He put two more bottles in my saddle-bag. Still there if you change your mind.'

'He's already got Mrs Hanson,' Jeff said bitterly, 'isn't that enough?'

Hanks grimaced. 'He wanted to

make sure of you. Rupe never trusts nobody, least of all a female. Figured she might back out on the deal once you'd got clear.'

Jeff stared at him. 'What do you mean? What deal?'

One malevolent eye squinted back at him. 'Nothin'. I don't mean nothin'.'

'Are you saying it was all a lie? That Rupe threatened her somehow?'

When Hanks didn't answer Jeff raised the .32 and clicked back the hammer. 'Put the jar down. Do it,' he rasped, as the man hesitated.

'Kneel. And take off your belt. Nice and slow. I'd say when a man's lost the sight of an eye he's in enough trouble, it's no time to be stopping a bullet. That's fine. Now lie down on your belly with your hands behind your back.'

Hanks cursed but he didn't try anything as Jeff strapped his hands together, turned him over and propped him up against a rock.

'That's better. Now I'll ask you again, and this time you're going to answer.' Jeff holstered the gun and picked up a branch from the remains of the fire.

'Funny how a man takes things for granted,' he said, waving the piece of wood in the air so the tip glowed red. He pointed it at Hanks's face. 'You spend thirty some years with two eyes, then you've only got one. A man has to learn to appreciate what he's got . . . '

'No!' Hanks screamed, throwing himself sideways, frantically trying to propel himself away. 'You can't . . . You wouldn't . . . '

Jeff crouched down, bringing the burning brand close to the man's face. 'You came close to choking me the other night. Why shouldn't I?'

'Don't . . . ' Hanks sobbed. 'Hell, I don't know much. Wouldn't know a thing only Rupe couldn't keep his mouth shut, he was so damn pleased with hisself. He told her to get rid of you; he swore you wouldn't live to see another day if she didn't. She was mild as milk, no arguin'. Guess she knew one man's got no chance against the Double Bar K outfit. Rupe was laughin' fit to bust about that tale she told you.'

There was a short silence as Jeff took in what he was hearing. 'She never let Rupe visit her at the Lazy Zee?'

'Hell no; only time he tried she threw him out. Wasn't his idea anyhow, he didn't want tyin' to no wife, he's got a couple of whores in Burville that suit him just fine. It was his pa, always had a hankerin' to get his hands on that parcel of land.'

Jeff turned away and picked up the stone jar. He swept it down hard against the rock that Hanks's back was propped against so it shattered into a dozen pieces, splashing the man's head.

'Rupe got what he wanted,' he said, hunkering down beside Hanks. 'How come he isn't heading for home? You said the posse would be coming by, but what about Rupe? No way is he going to stay out there and take his chances with Darbo against Cord's gang. The day'll never dawn when Rupe Krantz turns into a law-abiding citizen.'

Hanks hesitated. A slight smile curved Jeff's lips, but there was no trace of it in his eyes. 'Fire's still alight,' he said. 'Just in case you were thinking of telling me a lie.'

★   ★   ★

'That feel better?' Cassie Hanson gently eased Nate Grundy's leg down on the heap of blankets.

'It does. Thank you, ma'am.'

'I'll make up the fire.'

Nate stared at the dark sky. 'A couple of hours to daybreak. Guess you couldn't sleep either.'

She didn't answer, keeping her face turned away.

'Who's keeping watch on Hell's Gate?' he asked.

'The marshal. And Rupe Krantz is with him.' She glanced down the canyon towards the horse-line and let out a sigh.

'Mrs Hanson? There's something Eli

said. I'd sure be grateful if you could fill me in on what happened. Seems it maybe wasn't Jeff's fault when he missed riding with the posse the other day.'

She hesitated, but only for a moment. 'Rupe must have found out that Jeff was staying in town that night, at the livery. When Tree went to fetch my mare in the morning he found Jeff drunk, but there were rope marks round his wrists and anklcs, and he looked like he'd taken a beating. Tree said the Double Bar K hands forced two bottles of whiskey down his throat.'

'Anybody else see what happened?'

'I don't think so, but they tied up old Mr Lensky so he didn't interfere.'

Nate nodded. 'I'm glad Jeff didn't go back on his word. Maybe my spare Winchester didn't get hocked for a bottle after all.'

'Rupe's carrying a Winchester,' Cassie told him.

'That don't surprise me. Tell you the truth, it's not easy seeing Rupe Krantz as a member of this posse, it don't fit.'

Cassie said nothing, turning away.

'You should try for some sleep,' Nate said. 'It's a long ride back to Redemption.'

Once he was alone again Nate reached for the two sticks Eli had cut for him. Taking his weight on his arms did nothing for the knot of pain in his back, but he gritted his teeth as he swung his injured ankle forward and set off in the direction of Hell's Gate. Long before he got that far he had to admit defeat. He dropped to hands and knees, and dragged the crutches behind him, half-dizzy with pain.

A fire lit the high arch of stone, while two figures sat in the shadows against the canyon wall. Nate stopped to rest, watching them. He'd wait a while then heave himself up with the help of the cliff at his side; he wasn't going to let Darbo see him crawl. One of the men stood up to throw more fuel on the fire.

'You sure about this?' It was Rupe's voice, pitched low.

'Sure I'm sure. C'mon, kid, you've had enough of takin' orders from your pa. Seems to me you ain't eager to tie yourself to that woman neither. Can't say I blame you, the way she came taggin' along after Warrinder. If we pull this off you can do what you want; you'll have more money than your pa's ever seen.'

'It sounds tempting, but maybe they won't listen to you.'

'I told you, I know Steiger.' Darbo sounded suddenly sly. 'Besides, I got a message to him, from up on the ridge, threw it down after Kemp went over. Steiger's waitin' for us; all we gotta do is ride in there under a white flag an' make the deal.'

'What about the posse?'

'They'll be gone in a few hours. Grundy thinks Hanks rode to Saquiro Rock to fetch some troopers; he don't know you sent him after Warrinder. Hell, this is why I got rid of Kemp an' that dope from the stockyard, we ain't never gonna get another chance.

Steiger's real mad about Cord an' Brodie bringin' this crowd of hicks down on 'im.'

'But then they might not trust him,' Rupe protested. 'All three of us could get ourselves shot.'

'Not likely.' Darbo laughed. 'We got ourselves the prettiest little distraction you ever did see. Seein' as how you don't want her, reckon the little widow might as well make herself useful.'

'You really think Steiger will stand by and let you shoot down his partners?'

'Him an' Brodie rode together, but they ain't friends. We'll pitch him a fair deal; we'll only be takin' Brodie's share of the money.'

Nate groped for the sticks, knocking one of them against a stone. The sound of wood on rock was loud in the silence, setting up an echo.

'What was that?' Darbo was on his feet, staring down the canyon.

Face down in the dust, not even daring to breathe, Nate froze, waiting for the bullet that would end his life.

17

The horse's hoofs beat out a hectic rhythm as it galloped back towards the canyons. Jeff's head throbbed with every footfall but he hardly noticed, nor did he feel the sore heat of his burnt arm. Even his body's yearning for liquor was no more than a nagging at the back of his mind. He rode without seeing the miles unrolling before him, his head filled with images from another time. The memories had finally untangled.

He'd been a boy of just ten summers, sitting astride an old sway-backed mare, his rump jarring on its bony spine, his eyes scanning the ground as he followed the trail of some forty horses. The hoof marks weren't fresh; the riders had passed this way three days before.

Already he'd spent one night under

the stars, and he felt himself man enough for whatever adventures lay ahead. The leather bag slung round his neck still held a handful of biscuits and some hard tack, and the canteen bumping against his ribs was full.

As the sun rose higher and the old horse tired, the boy rode and walked by turns. A storm might have stopped him, bringing rain to wash out the tracks, but the sky was clear over the mountains, and the air carried no scent of a change. There was a sound rolling in the far distance but it wasn't thunder.

The noise rarely ceased, growing louder as the day wore on. Following the tracks, finding wheel marks showing here and there in the dust, that younger Jeff Warrinder had made the best speed he could. A thrashing would be the likely welcome he'd get from his father, but with only a couple of miles to go the boy pushed the reluctant horse to a gallop, eager to get there, only afraid that he'd be too late.

When the man leapt out of nowhere to block their path the old mare shied wildly. A second before the landscape had been deserted; it seemed as if an apparition had jumped out of solid rock. Flung over the horse's shoulder, Jeff somersaulted, slamming down hard on his back with the wind driven out of him.

His memory was hazy for a while then. A stranger's face looked into his. He saw a skinny young man with pale hair, and skin burnt red by the sun. There was a bloody scrape down his cheek, where downy fluff might one day grow into a beard. The man's shirt, grey with dust, was torn at the shoulder. Despite his confusion, Jeff's mind had come up with a name. This had to be Billy Meacher.

'Feelin' better?'

Water trickled into Jeff's mouth and he choked then nodded. 'I'm fine.'

He'd struggled to sit up, staring round in an attempt to locate the old mare. Only a cloud of dust showed where she was, travelling fast and far off alongside the looming cliff.

'Horse knows where it's goin',' the young man said, 'how about you?'

Jeff paused for only a second before deciding to tell the truth. 'My pa's with the posse. I followed the troopers from town. I've never seen artillery before, not even practising.'

'An' I bet you want to get yourself a look at them wicked outlaws. Well, you got your wish, boy. Guess you know who I am. Ain't much like that picture they peg up, am I? Jed an' Harve got the looks, I got the brains.' Billy Meacher shrugged. 'Either one of 'em would have slit your throat, just for bein' here. An' they'd have been real mad about losin' that horse of yours. I got a powerful long walk ahead of me.'

Jeff looked into the pale-blue eyes. He'd seen death a couple of times, but had never considered his own. It seemed unreal, too unlikely to worry about. He returned Billy Meacher's look, unblinking and unafraid.

'You're supposed to be scared.' The sunburnt face cracked into a smile. 'Guess you got lucky. I ain't Jed an' I ain't Harve. Fact is I never killed nobody, an' I ain't startin' now, not with a kid. You believe me, doncha?'

Jeff nodded. 'Did you climb down from up there?' He asked, staring at the sheer face of the cliff.

'Nope. Not down. There's another way. Wasn't none too easy. Sure wish . . . ' His eyes clouded for a moment, then he shrugged. 'Your pa's gonna be ridin' back here like the devil hisself once your horse comes in.'

Meacher got to his feet. 'I better get movin'. Least I'm travellin' light.' He slapped at the six-gun at his hip, which was all he carried.

'Wait.' Jeff pulled the bag over his head and tipped out the contents. 'I can't give you the bag, because my pa would notice, but you can take the rest. He'll just call me a darn fool for coming out without enough to last me.'

Billy Meacher hesitated no more than

a moment, then he stuffed the food inside his shirt. 'Thanks.'

Jeff dragged at the strap of the canteen, but the young man shook his head.

'I know every water-hole from here to the border. And they won't be lookin' for me, not unless you tell 'em what happened.'

'I won't,' Jeff promised, rising to his feet. 'I swear it. I hope you get away.'

Billy Meacher grinned, 'Thanks. So long, kid.' Within minutes he was out of sight, leaving nothing but the prints of his worn boots behind.

★ ★ ★

Maybe a minute passed, but to Nate, lying in the dust half suffocating, it felt like an hour. At last he heard the murmur of voices, but pitched lower this time. He couldn't make out what Rupe and Darbo were saying, but it hardly mattered, he'd heard enough. Pulling the crutches close to him, he began to inch very slowly back the way he'd come. His ankle felt as if it was on fire, and something warm and wet trickled down his back; the wound had opened up again.

Nate bit his lip as his toes caught on a stone. He couldn't afford to make a sound; if the two men knew he'd overheard them he'd be out of pain real soon; Eli would be digging a hole for him alongside Morrissey.

The dim glow of embers crept gradually nearer. He was close to exhausted. His bedroll was only ten yards away, but he didn't think he was going to make it. Around the remains of the fire, dark shapes showed where the rest of the posse slept, wrapped up against the night chill.

Nate was dripping sweat. He lay still a while, gathering his strength. Taking the sticks in one hand he reached with the other, clawing at the rock face to heave himself up, somehow getting his good foot to the ground.

The camp-fire looked too far. Up

towards Hell's Gate he saw movement. Darbo and Rupe were coming. Nate launched himself out from the cliff face, away from the incriminating trail he'd left; even a child could have read the marks in the dust. He managed six tottering steps before he fell. An idea struck him and he turned, away from the sleeping men, away from the camp. With luck they would think he'd been heading further into the canyon, coming to look for the men keeping watch beneath the great stone arch, not intent on getting away from them.

The ground came up at him uncomfortably fast, and there was no time to release his hold on the sticks to save himself. He could only roll and take some of the impact on his shoulder, but still his head struck hard. After the knock it had taken less than twenty-four hours before this was too much. Nate dropped into darkness.

★　★　★

Recalling himself to the present Jeff slowed the horse to a walk and stared along the towering wall of stone, trying to see it with the eyes of the boy he'd been. Twenty years was a long time, but he was sure this was the place. He hadn't lingered that day, knowing Billy Meacher was right, his father would come searching for him when the mare galloped into the canyons, drawn there by the scent of other horses. Having given his promise he put as much distance as he could between himself and the place where the young man had come down out of the mountain.

Jeff stared at the cliff, facing north to squint towards the canyon's entrance a couple of miles away, then south to look back the way he'd come. This was the exact spot where he'd encountered Billy Meacher. He climbed from the saddle and hitched the horse to a rock.

Closing his eyes, feeling the heat of the sun on his skin, Jeff tried to relive that moment when the young man had appeared, as if he'd dropped out of the sky . . .

That was it. He'd come from above. Jeff scanned the rock face, moving away from it to get a clearer view. There was something, hardly long enough or wide enough to be called a ledge, maybe fifteen foot above the ground. From closer in it was invisible.

Jeff led the horse to the spot and tossed down a few handfuls of grain. He put the saddle-bags over his shoulder and lifted on to the horse's back, then slow and easy, talking to the animal while it ate, he got to his feet, standing on the saddle, looking for places to put his feet.

The rock was worn smooth by years of wind and rain. Narrow cracks ran down its surface, not wide enough to fit the toe of his boot. At last he lifted his foot, and jammed it sideways into the widest gap. Taking his weight on that leg he reached as high as he could with questing fingers, found another crack and hauled himself up. He'd forgotten that Rupe had broken a couple of his toes until he tried the same manoeuvre with the other foot. Just one more score to settle, he told himself, gritting his teeth.

It took him two minutes but it felt like ten. He hoisted himself on to the narrow shelf of rock, staring at the dark slit before him, three feet high and not much more than a foot across. He stared up and around. This had to be it, there was nothing else. Kneeling down he pushed a hand into the gap and felt the dusty floor, and the space that seemed to widen out behind the narrow opening. He pushed the saddle-bags through, then scrunched up his shoulders and dived into the dark.

★   ★   ★

Nate came back to consciousness. The world was moving uncomfortably, jolting his injured leg and setting up a throb around his backbone. A moan escaped him and the motion stopped.

'Hey, Eli, he's comin' around!' Shorty Sims's moon-shaped face was the first thing he saw, the big man grinning down at him. 'We was worried, Sheriff, you sure did sleep some.'

'Sleep!' Eli Ranovich snorted. 'Been out cold for near ten hours. Tomfool thing to do, tryin' to go marchin' around in the middle of the night. I thought you wasn't gonna come around nohow, figured to get you back to the doc, if you wasn't dead first.'

Pushing up on his elbows Nate looked at the men and horses around him. 'Darbo's not here? Or Rupe?'

'Nossir. They're waitin' for the troopers,' Jim Ormond said. 'Marshal ain't got time for us townfolk, he couldn't get us cleared out fast enough.'

'What about Mrs Hanson? She still with them?'

'She wouldn't leave,' Eli said, a frown adding more lines to his wrinkled face. 'Said she'd stay with Rupe. Couldn't see no way to force her if she wanted it that way.'

'Dammit!' Nate grabbed at the crutches that lay alongside him on the travois and rolled himself onto the ground. 'We have to go back. Jeff'll go crazy . . . '

'Jeff? He'll be nigh on back to town by now.' Shorty's big hands hauled Nate Grundy on to the travois again.

'Ain't no good interferin', Nate,' Eli put in. 'The woman made her own choice.'

'Will you listen?' Nate said desperately. 'I heard Darbo talking to Rupe last night. There aren't any troopers coming. Hanks didn't go to Saquiro Rock, he went after Jeff Warrinder.'

'That's crazy. Darbo an' Rupe can't deal with them coyotes on their own.' Eli shook his head, looking worried. 'You'd best take it easy, Sheriff. A knock on the head can do strange things to a man's mind. Joe, you got anythin' left in that flask?'

'I'll give you a knock on the head if you don't see sense.' Nate sat up, ignoring the sharp stab from the wound in his back. 'Since when did one of the Krantz family ever take the law's side in anything? Darbo knows Steiger, the man who was in the canyon before the others arrived. I tell you, the marshal's selling out. Handing Jeff over could be part of the bargain; Brodie's real keen to see him dead. Then there's Cassie Hanson . . . '

He couldn't bring himself to spell it out. 'She may not be safe with Rupe. Listen to me dammit! At least send a rider to look for Jeff.'

'Figure we can do that,' Eli said.

'Could be he's still at the water-hole. Looks like somebody left a fire burnin', there's smoke comin' up,' Herb Osmond said. 'Maybe he's waitin' for us.'

'Joe, you an' Jim got the fastest horses,' Eli said.

'The rest of us'll follow quick as we can,' Nate said. 'And will somebody help get me off this damn thing and on to my horse?'

18

'Jeff ain't there,' Jim Ormond shouted as he spurred back to Nate and the rest of the posse. 'Just Hanks. Seems him and Jeff tangled some.'

'How d'you mean, tangled?' Nate asked.

'Wouldn't have believed if I hadn't seen it,' Jim replied. 'Jeff put one of Hanks's eyes out while he'd got him tied up. Joe stayed to see if he could help any, he'll be right along.'

Nate frowned. 'Jeff did that? Eli, if the man's hurt bad maybe you better go see — '

'Nope. Nothin' I can do.' Eli was blunt. 'An' I'd need to hear Jeff's side of the story before I took Hanks's word on it. Said yourself he ain't a man you'd want at your back. Question is, where'd Jeff go?'

'Accordin' to Hanks he was headin' back to the canyons. He's spittin' mad at Rupe,' Jim Ormond said. 'Real strange we didn't meet him.'

'Maybe that's the way he wanted it. Maybe Hanks told him what Rupe and Darbo had in mind.' Nate dragged his horse's head around. 'Come on.'

★ ★ ★

Jeff crouched in the dark and buckled down the flap of the saddle-bags; it was no time to be careless. He lit the piece of slow match he'd cut.

The glow of the fuse gave a meagre light, showing only the nearest couple of feet of rock. Already crouching under the roof as it dipped towards the floor, Jeff got down on hands and knees, pushing the saddle-bags in front of him. Soon he was on his belly, snaking along the ground and still in danger of knocking his brains out.

A spike of rock snatched at his shirt and ripped it from neck to waist, then his holster caught on some unseen obstacle and he had to unbuckle it to get free. He laid the .32 on top of the saddle-bags. This was why Billy Meacher had been alone that day. Jeff had seen the posters in the sheriff's office; the other Meacher brothers must have weighed more than 220 apiece, they never would have made it through.

The piece of slow match burned down to his fingers. Jeff struck a light again to look further ahead, staring at the tiny space. He swallowed hard. It didn't look possible.

With a fresh length of fuse alight in his hand he inched forward, bracing with his feet, his shoulders scraping against rock on either side. The second length of slow match was almost at an end. Jeff felt for the spare piece he'd tucked into the front of his shirt. It wasn't there.

He didn't let go of the fuse until it scorched his fingers. A moment later the darkness descended, falling over him like a blanket. He told himself it made no difference. What was the point of seeing when there was so little to see?

Jeff bit down hard on his lip. Some-where up ahead was the way out. And Cassie. By now she was probably alone with Rupe and Darbo.

Jeff fought against the panic that snagged at his mind, as the rocks snagged at his flesh, drawing blood. It felt as if he'd spent a lifetime trapped here in the dark, accompanied only by his heart's frantic pounding.

Then he heard voices. Distant, distorted, but unmistakable. He slith-ered through a gap so narrow that his shoulders jammed. Breathing slow he eased one arm back and thrust forward again. He got through at the cost of a few more scraps of skin.

Abruptly the tunnel was wider and higher, and the darkness wasn't quite so black. Far ahead was a tiny light, there was floor visible beneath him and the roof above. He no longer had to crawl like some blind cave dwelling insect, he could stand and walk like a man. Cautious, the sound of voices ebbing and flowing in his ears, Jeff crept towards the daylight.

Halting near the opening, he undid the saddle-bags and took out the sticks of explosive, already bound in bundles. Until he knew exactly what he was going to find he wasn't sure how he might use them, but he trimmed fuses to different lengths and attached them in readiness; the shortest would burn for less than a minute, the longest for five times that. He put his makeshift weapons back into the saddle-bag, but this time he didn't buckle down the flap.

★　★　★

'Come on.' Rupe Krantz took Cassie by the arm and dragged her to her feet.

'Where are we going?' she asked, trying to pull away. 'I thought we were staying here until the troopers came.'

'You thought wrong.' He hurried her towards Hell's Gate. 'But then you got it all wrong, lady. You didn't really think I'd take you for a wife just to get my hands on that run-down spread? That's no kind of a bargain.'

'You . . . ' Her face paled. 'Then why did you make me tell all those lies to Jeff?'

'For the look on Warrinder's face.' Rupe laughed. 'Sure was a picture.'

'You bastard!' She swung on him but he kept hold of her arm and twisted it savagely.

'I've had enough of your tongue,' he said, wrenching her hand up behind her back. 'If I didn't have a use for you I swear I'd cut that pretty little throat.'

He jerked her arm again and Cassie cried out in pain.

'Hush up. Come on, Darbo's waiting.' He shoved her in front of him, out into the open space beyond the great rock arch, across the killing ground where Nate Grundy had fallen and on up the rough track towards the outlaws' hideout.

Marshal Darbo stood with the four outlaws by the mouth of a huge cave. Rupe pushed Cassie away from him so she almost fell at Ross Cord's feet.

'Well, lookee here.' The outlaw grinned.

'You told me you'd got Warrinder,' Brodie said, glaring at Darbo. 'I don't see him.'

'He's down the trail with one of my men,' Rupe said. 'Head south and follow the smell of whiskey.'

'I had him once,' Brodie growled, 'until that little hellcat pushed him into the river. We figured they was both drowned.'

'But we got lucky.' That was Cord. He ran a thumbnail down Cassie's cheek. 'Here's our little rustler, an' just as pretty as ever.'

She slapped him hard, leaving finger marks. He laughed. 'Just as sassy, too.'

'Let's deal,' Darbo said. 'You boys ride out an' me an' Krantz'll see the posse don't come after you. All we ask is somethin' for our trouble.' He gave Steiger a sidelong glance. 'Maybe two thousand apiece? We'll throw in the little widow woman an' the drunk for nothin'.'

'Hold it.' Brodie turned on Cord. 'I

told you I didn't want no woman along when we broke you out of jail, an' that ain't changed none.'

'Fine,' Cord replied. 'I ain't arguin'. Go find the man who killed your brother, if that's what you want.'

'Not till I know the posse's gone.'

'I'll see to that,' Darbo said. 'Soon as we get the money.'

'You goin' for this?' Brodie asked suspiciously, looking at Steiger.

'Why not?' Steiger jerked his head at Darbo. 'Me and the marshal go back a long way. Come and fetch him the money, Brodie. Rest of you can have yourselves some fun with the little lady.' He leered at Cassie then turned to go into the cave.

'I'd rather see this gets played fair,' Mac said. 'The woman can wait. What d'you say, Cord?'

'I been real lonesome. Couldn't stop thinkin' about this little honey. Reckon I trust you boys.' Cord took Cassie by the arm, digging his fingers into her flesh.

'Sure would like to see what you look like under them men's clothes.'

'Why don't the three of us go someplace more comfortable,' Rupe said, taking hold of Cassie on the other side.

'Sure.' Cord nodded, licking his lips. 'There's plenty of caves, real nice and homey.'

Cassie was helpless. They dragged her uphill and under a high arch of rock. In a dark narrow cave they threw her down on the dirt floor.

'Take them clothes off,' Cord said thickly.

'No.' She was free for a few seconds, grasping desperately at the knife at her waist, but Rupe was too quick for her, capturing her fingers and squeezing them until she dropped the weapon. Grinning widely he wrestled her to the ground. He knelt, holding her arms out to the sides and jamming the top of her head against his knees.

'That's better,' he said, glancing up at the outlaw. 'Seeing she's shy why don't you give her a helping hand?'

Cord was breathing fast. He knelt beside Cassie to pull away her coat, ripping at the shirt underneath, his hands clumsy in his excitement.

Cassie kicked him, screaming defiance.

'Ain't no way to behave,' Cord said. He caught hold of her legs and trapped them beneath him. Panting, laughing in triumph, he unbuckled the leather belt at her waist.

'Get on with it,' Rupe urged roughly.

'Hell, a woman's supposed to wear skirts, not wrap herself up like . . . ' Cord's voice faded into silence at the sight of her pale nakedness lying on the dirt floor.

The outlaw swallowed hard, fumbling to undo his pants. 'I was right,' he said. 'I knew you'd be worth takin' along.'

A dark shape erupted through the mouth of the cave, a fist swinging to take Cord on the side of the head and lift him clear off the ground. Another punch took the man on the jaw and his skull hit the rock wall with a thud.

Jeff Warrinder turned to deal with Rupe Krantz, fists clenched. Then he stopped, gulping in air, the colour draining from his face.

'Only takes a move,' Rupe said softly, 'and she's as dead as your wife, Warrinder.' He had Cassie's head in a wrestler's grip between his hands, the powerful fingers holding tight. Jeff stopped breathing. He took a step back, then another.

'Very wise. Now, unless you want me to break this pretty little neck, you'll put your head out there and shout for Brodie.' Rupe smiled. 'Good and loud.'

Jeff obeyed, his voice cracking. He took a step back towards Rupe. 'Don't . . . ' he begged, his eyes never leaving Rupe's triumphant face.

A tiny crack of sound came from somewhere outside. At the very instant when the makeshift bomb exploded, splitting apart the rock above the outlaws' cave further down the hill, Jeff launched himself at Rupe, a great flying leap that carried him over Cord's corpse to land on Cassie's naked body, his two fists smashing down at Rupe's arms with every ounce of his weight behind them.

Everything went dark as the ground shook and rumbled. The air was thick with dust and Rupe Krantz's scream was barely audible above the thunder of falling rock.

Jeff rolled off Cassie, not knowing if she was dead or alive, terrified that he'd killed her. Rupe followed, somehow taking a grip on Jeff's throat with his right hand; the left was useless, the elbow joint a ruin of red flesh and broken white bone. Jeff pummelled at Rupe with his fists, hitting hard, but the fingers around his neck went on getting tighter.

'Jeff.' Cassie's voice reached him through the red fog that was descending on his brain. She was alive.

Jeff Warrinder groped for Rupe's injured arm, found it and took a hold, heaving hard. Rupe's face, hanging above him in the gloom, contorted with a mix of rage and pain. The pressure on Jeff's windpipe slackened and he dragged in a breath. With every ounce of strength left in his body he slammed a punch at Rupe's exposed throat. He felt something give way under his fist and Rupe collapsed on top of him.

'Jeff,' Cassie said again, her voice urgent. He pushed Rupe off him and got up. A man stood in the entrance to the cave, a Winchester in his hands.

Brodie smiled. 'Hello, Warrinder.'

* * *

A great boom rent the air as the posse rode back into the campsite they'd left early that morning. It sounded as if the canyons were collapsing around their ears. The blast hit them a second later, a hot wind driving down through Hell's Gate, dust flaying bare skin on hands and faces.

'Jeez, what was that?' Shorty Sims cried.

'Jeff Warrinder,' Nate replied grimly, kicking back hard with his sound leg. Now he knew what Al Green had given to Jeff when he called in that favour. 'I should've figured it out. Come on!'

They raced up the canyon unopposed. At the head of the slope the outlaws' terrified horses plunged and squealed. A man was staggering blindly towards them, clutching at a bloody wound to his head.

'That's Darbo.' Herb Ormond and Shorty Sims leapt from their horses and grabbed him; the marshal was too dazed to argue. He let himself be led over to Nate.

'Sheriff. Glad you're here. I . . . '

'Marshal,' Nate returned. 'Be obliged if you'd turn your weapon over to my men.' Darbo started to protest, but found himself staring down the barrel of Eli's rifle.

They found another man, or part of one. The cave mouth had gone, replaced by a great rock slide. A hand stuck out from underneath. When

Shorty pulled at it an arm came free, ending in shattered bone and red rags of flesh.

'Where's Jeff Warrinder?' Nate demanded, easing down from his horse and clinging to the saddle bow. Darbo stared blankly at him. Nate grabbed the marshal's shirt front and shook him. 'Who was in there?'

'Steiger an' Mac,' Darbo replied, glancing at the bloody remnant in Shorty's hand.

'What about Mrs Hanson?'

'Krantz and Cord took her.'

Eli thrust the rifle barrel into Darbo's ribs. 'You didn't see Jeff?' the old man snarled.

'Warrinder?' Darbo's mouth dropped open. 'How could he get in here?'

'The same way Billy Meacher got out,' Nate replied grimly. 'Only it looks like Jeff closed the door behind him. Where did they take Mrs Hanson? Show us.'

Darbo pointed to a deep shadowed cleft. 'They called Brodie up there, just before it happened.'

There was movement within the shadows. 'Take cover,' Nate said, pushing Darbo behind a rock.

Naked to the waist, Jeff Warrinder walked out of the cave with his hands held high. Behind him was a small figure dressed only in boots and the tattered ruins of a man's shirt. Brodie followed, holding a Winchester.

The last stone rolled over the grave of Mac and Steiger, and the day was still.

'That's far enough, Warrinder,' Brodie said. 'Turn around an' say goodbye to your little whore.'

A shot blasted the silence. Slowly, Jeff Warrinder turned, his eyes dead in an expressionless face. Before he could take in the fact that Cassie Hanson was still alive, she was in his arms. Smoke drifted up from the barrel of Eli's old rifle as Brodie fell.

What was left of the posse came whooping up the slope, Nate carried between Shorty and Jim. Eli stumped along at the back, not taking his gaze off Brodie until he was close enough to see that his bullet had taken the outlaw between the eyes.

'Nice shot,' Nate conceded. 'Reckon Jeff'll want to keep you on as deputy when he's sheriff again.'

'That'll be never,' Jeff said. He grinned, one filthy hand caressing Cassie's hair. 'I'm going to marry a wealthy widow and get me a ranch.'

THE END

We do hope that you have enjoyed reading this large print book.

Did you know that all of our titles are available for purchase?

We publish a wide range of high quality large print books including:
Romances, Mysteries, Classics
General Fiction
Non Fiction and Westerns

Special interest titles available in large print are:
The Little Oxford Dictionary
Music Book, Song Book
Hymn Book, Service Book

Also available from us courtesy of Oxford University Press:
Young Readers' Dictionary
(large print edition)
Young Readers' Thesaurus
(large print edition)

For further information or a free brochure, please contact us at:
Ulverscroft Large Print Books Ltd.,
The Green, Bradgate Road, Anstey,
Leicester, LE7 7FU, England.
Tel: (00 44) **0116 236 4325**
Fax: (00 44) **0116 234 0205**

LAWMAN'S LAMENT

David Bingley

When Judge Jonathan B. Lacey is killed in an ambush in Big Springs County, Texas, his dying words to town marshal Dan Marden alter the course of Dan's life. Quitting his work as marshal, Dan embarks upon a hunt for Lacey's murderers, the outlaw Long John Verne and his gang. Then Dan's brother Vance becomes involved in running battles between towns, making Dan's task almost impossible. Now the ex-marshal must struggle to complete his quest.

THE DYING TREE

Edward Thomson

With the railroad pushing into Indian territory, the peace treaty between the Sioux and the white men is broken. Sioux warriors attack railroad surveyors and only Civil War veteran Mike Wilson escapes. Serving his own purposes, the railroad boss schemes for an Indian war, which triggers an explosive and violent reaction from the local tribes. Now there would be war lasting for many years, drenching the prairie grass with the blood of Indians and white men alike.

FURY AT TROON'S FERRY

Mark Bannerman

In the gathering darkness he strode purposefully up the empty street. The only sounds came from the saloon; men's raucous voices and the shrill laughter of women. His wife, Leah, had once said that nothing was achieved by violence . . . But now he was convinced that she was wrong, and his desire was to inflict vengeance. Before bullets started flying, as surely they must, would he be able to extract the truth from the man he sought . . . and despised?